P9-CQC-761

ANNEXED

SHARON DOGAR

HOUGHTON MIFFLIN

HOUGHTON MIFFLIN HARCOURT

BOSTON   NEW YORK 2010

TO JEM, XA, AND ELLA,

OUR CHILDREN.

THIS IS FOR YOU.

THANK YOU.

*May you never lay your head
down without a hand to hold . . .*

Copyright © 2010 by Sharon Dogar

First published in 2010 by Andersen Press Limited
20 Vauxhall Bridge Road, London SW1V 2SA
www.andersenpress.co.uk

All rights reserved. For information about permission to
reproduce selections from this book, write to Permissions,
Houghton Mifflin Harcourt Publishing Company,
215 Park Avenue South, New York, New York 10003.

Houghton Mifflin is an imprint of Houghton Mifflin
Harcourt Publishing Company.

Library of Congress cataloging-in-publication data is on file.
ISBN 978-0-547-50195-6

The right of Sharon Dogar to be identified as the author of this work
has been asserted by her in accordance with the Copyright, Designs,
and Patents Act, 1988.

Manufactured in the United States of America
DOC 10 9 8 7 6 5 4 3
4500280062

Preface

It is nearly five months into 1945. The Second World War is about to end. Peter van Pels is in a Nazi concentration camp called Mauthausen. He is recorded as having been admitted to the sick bay there on April 11. This would mean he was in the sick bay for more than three weeks, which is either inaccurate or extraordinary. No one who had survived the Nazi occupation of Holland, a transport to Auschwitz, the walk through Poland and Austria to Mauthausen, and then "worked" for three months, could be expected to survive for more than a few days at most in a sick bay—which was really just a river of dying people passing through. There was no treatment, and barely any food—not at this stage of the war.

But extraordinary stories of survival against all odds happened again and again throughout the Holocaust, so what if it was true? What if, while he is lying in the sick bay, Peter begins, in memory, to travel through his short life? He is eighteen. He has spent two of those eighteen years in the "Annex" in Amsterdam: a place made famous by Anne Frank's diary. But what was it like for Peter?

In this novel, based on history, I try to imagine what it might have been like to have actually lived with Anne Frank. To become the target of her love, and to be so cruelly torn apart from her, just as liberation was coming to Holland.

Part of what is so heartbreaking about the story of Anne Frank and her family and friends in the attic is that they so very, very nearly survived and made it through to the end of the war. They were on the last train into Auschwitz from Holland. In the end, only one of them made it, Otto Frank, Anne's beloved father.

As I write this, Anne Frank (if still alive) would have only been in her eighties. She might still be writing stories, still be reminding us of what it means to stay alive to the beauty of the world when all around you lies evidence of death, hatred, and destruction.

But for all her unique intelligence and aliveness, Anne did not live her life with the knowledge that one day she would become an icon. She was a fiercely passionate, intelligent, contemptuous, and, at times, difficult young woman. Otto Frank said, publicly, that he "did not know" the Anne Frank that everyone feels they know so well from her diary, and that from this he must deduce one simple thing: "that as parents we do not know our children." Any "imaginary" account of what happened in the Annex should take note of this statement from Anne's father. The Anne seen in her diary is not necessarily the same Anne that the people in the attic felt they knew.

And what of Peter? Does the Peter that Anne writes about bear any resemblance to who Peter really was? What's it like to be in someone else's diary (especially one so famous), pinned down for all time as seen through the eyes of someone else? What if Peter, as Anne suggests several times, wasn't at all as she thought?

The way we see both people and history can change over time. Anne's diary is a vitally important part of our history. It tells us in some detail what it was like to live in hiding during the Nazi occupation and "cleansing" of Holland. The facts of the Holocaust are not something writers should play with, but what we *can* do is reimagine the story of what happened between the people in the Annex—and how they felt about each other. How do we know what Anne would say about it all now, if she could? She would almost certainly feel more charitable toward her mother and Fritz Pfeffer. What we feel as adolescents can be both powerful and passionate, but it is not the only truth.

And what would the others have to say about her portrayal of them—especially Peter? This is what I've imagined. How it might all have felt from Peter's point of view. I have done my best not to change the facts of their existence in the Annex, or (in as far as it is possible to know) what happened after they left the Annex and entered the world of the Nazi death camps.

Reimagining can be an important part of keeping history alive, and there was no one more acutely alive, clever, and curious about the world than Anne Frank. Sadly, we can't change what happened to her and her family and friends. But we can keep on telling her story, keep on thinking about what it means to be human, in both our love and our hatred for ourselves—and we can (as Anne Frank has) try to keep the facts of what happened during the Second World War alive for each new generation, in the hope that they remain aware of how catastrophic the consequences of hate can be.

Prologue

MAY 1945 — PETER: AUSTRIA, MAUTHAUSEN, SICK BAY

I think I'm still alive.

But I'm not sure.

I'm ill.

I must be because I'm lying down. We never lie down.

In the camps there's no such thing as rest.

I should be carrying rocks up the quarry steps. It's a long way to the top of the quarry. I never know if I will make it. If someone ahead of us falls, we all fall—unless we're quick.

Sometimes the guards wait until one of us is on the very last step, already thinking of laying down his burden, of the relief of letting down the weight. That's when they reach out with their boots and kick us down. We fall like dominoes.

That's all I remember, falling down the side of the quarry. I feel my body jolt and bounce. I feel the other bodies land on me. I am crushed, bony body on bony body. We are all so sharp now. My bones crunch. I am suffocating. The bodies move off me, the dead pushed aside by the living. I can breathe. My bones click back into place. I am alive and must get up, or I will be piled up with the dead. I try to stand.

I can see why the guards laugh. I look like a puppet. A puppet of bones with his strings all cut. I stand. I walk. I go on. But I know that really I am still dead on the ground, that each day a piece of us dies.

And we let it die. We have to—to survive.

Soon someone will come and wake me and the nightmare will begin.

I'm waiting for the word, that word:

WYSTAWACH.

Wake up.

If they come, then I must stand up and work, or I must die.

Perhaps I am already dying.

Everyone does in the end, there's no other way out.

And now it's my turn.

It's a relief.

The problem with lying down is that it brings memories. They keep on coming, reminding me of who I am.

The world.

My life.

The German Jews have a word for it.

Heimweh.

The longing for home. We avoid it if we can. It can be fatal.

I am hot. My head aches. My body hurts. These are just words, they don't explain the pain. The way my bones grind against each other. There are no words for pain like this.

But the memories are worse—pictures of a time before. Of a time I must deny, so that when they come to wake me I can go on. Put one foot in front of the other, pretending that there is only this moment, this day, this night to get through—and survive.

To tell my story.

But the memories persist; they push at the edges of my resistance. They spill.

There was a girl, wasn't there? There was a place.

A place where the leaves fell like golden coins from a tree into the water as we watched through the attic window . . . and before that there was a home, a street, a world, a girl I loved . . .

PART 1:
The Annex

I'm running through the streets; it's early morning and the sun tries to break through the mist. My footsteps echo. My thoughts race: *I'm not going into hiding. I'm not going into hiding—especially not with the Franks!*

I don't know where I'll go; I only know that I can't do it. I can't stay locked up in a tiny apartment with two girls (especially not Anne Frank) and Mutti and Mrs. Frank! Just because Father does business with them doesn't mean we have to like them! I'd rather take my chances on the streets.

My feet hit the pavement. Somewhere behind me there's the sound of an engine. I know at once what it is. We all know the sound—a military vehicle.

I slow down, keep to the shadows. It's still curfew time for Jews, not that I look like a Jew.

I'm nearly there.

At Liese's house.

"Liese."

I whisper her name. I imagine her face, her violet eyes and her soft dark hair. I imagine what she might do when I tell her I'm running. She might hold me; she might lie down in the grass with me. She might . . .

I need to concentrate. I need to get over the wall and into her back garden.

I take a run and try to vault it. It's high. I miss.

The sound of the engine comes closer.

I hit the wall with my left foot, and with fear fueling my fist I grab the top of it with my right hand—and this time I make it.

I drop onto the grass. Breathe hard and reach around me feeling for a stone, a twig, anything I can throw at her window to wake her.

But something stops me. I listen. The streets are silent. There's no sound. That means the engine's stopped. I stand completely still. Did they see me? Are they searching through the streets right now, listening, waiting for me to give myself away—to make a sound?

Into the silence comes a banging, a crashing of fists on the door and voices shouting.

"Open up! Open up!"

I stand in the garden, frozen. I watch as the lights come on. I see Liese's face appear briefly behind the window as she draws back the curtains—then she's gone. I watch as the whole family reappears behind the lit-up window of the sitting room. They're wearing their nightclothes. They gesticulate, argue, but in the end they pack their cases, put on their coats, and disappear—with Liese.

I know they're calling up teenage girls. I know that's why we're going into hiding, because Margot Frank has been called up. But I never thought it would happen to Liese.

I try to run to her, but my legs won't move; my hand's still behind me holding the stone. I don't know how long it is before I can move again, before I vault the wall and run to the corner of the street, but I know it's too late. The van's already moving. I watch it turn the corner and speed away.

With Liese in it.

I start to run. I run hard but the van's already racing down the street.

Liese!

Liese!

The van goes on, disappearing. I keep on running until I'm on my knees. Too late.

Too late.

She's gone.

I can't believe it. Why? Why her? Why now?

I turn back to the house. The door's locked but I know where the key's kept. Slowly, I unlock the door. Everything is neat and tidy. The piano lid is open—Liese's favorite piece of music is on the stand. Everything looks the same, but the house is empty of her and so everything is completely different. Where have they taken her—and why did they take all of them? Where shall I go now?

4

I don't know what to do.

I look out the window onto the street. I look at my watch. Six twenty-two. I'm meant to be at Mr. Frank's workplace in a few hours. We're arriving separately, all of us. We'll walk into the building just like it was any other visit—only this time we'll never walk out again.

We'll stay in there.

We don't know for how long.

I stare out the window.

The early-morning streets are empty, and so am I. I can't think of anything—except the van disappearing, and the fact that I stood there and let it happen! How did I ever think I could escape them, or fight them?

She's gone.

And I know what I'm doing.

I'm going into hiding.

I wait and watch as the streets fill with people. I wait and watch the sun get higher. I wait and watch the world come to life. I wait knowing that I'm not running anywhere because there's nowhere to run to.

I look out the window.

The world I can see isn't my world anymore—it's theirs: the National Socialist German Workers' Party's—the Nazis'. They've taken it away from me—piece by piece. I can't ride in trams or cars like everybody else. I can't swim in the same water or sit and watch films in the same cinema. I can't shop in gentile shops. I can't sit in the street. I can't drink from the water fountains. I can't walk anywhere without a star on my chest. I can't . . . I can't . . . I can't do anything. If someone decides to attack me I can't expect any help—and I mustn't fight back. If I *do,* then they might beat me to death, and no one would stop them. If I *don't* fight back, then I'm exactly what they say I am—a cowardly Jew-boy.

I don't exist anymore. They've turned me into a nobody so that they can wipe me off the face of the earth.

It feels so obvious to me now.

I can't believe I didn't see it before.

How did I miss it?

How did I ever think I could escape?

How did I ever think I could fight?

I should leave now. It's time. I find a satchel and a spare jacket with a star sewn onto it, but then at the last minute I decide not to wear it. If this is my last walk through the city I'm going to do it free—as me—and if anything happens, if they find me—then let them.

The walk to Prinsengracht is a long way, maybe an hour. At the end of it is a warehouse; at the top of the warehouse, hidden at the back, is an annex.

No one knows it's there, except the workers who'll help hide us. Father says we're lucky, lucky he happens to be in business with Mr. Frank. Lucky Mr. Frank's asked us to join his family in hiding. I don't think so. I'd rather be in America.

I've got a diagram of the Annex. I know where to go in, which stairs I have to use, and how to find my way to the back of the house where the rooms are hidden. Where *I'll* be hidden.

I should go now.

If I'm going.

I'm on the street. The sun is on my face. There is no star on my chest. I'm free for another hour. One more hour. The whole world feels strange around me: pin-sharp and beautiful. Without my star I get no pitying looks. I've forgotten what it's like not to be noticed. I stop. I drink from a fountain. Mutti would be horrified. I could be arrested, killed, sent away if I was found out. A Jew, drinking from a fountain! I could infect all the non-Jews, but with what?

What is it we've got that's so evil?

"Beautiful morning!" a woman says, and smiles. I smile back, but inside I'm thinking, *I'm a Jew, you stupid woman, can't you see? Can't you even tell what I am without my star to guide you? Here,* I think of saying to her, *put it on. If you feel so sorry for us why don't you all wear them, and then who would know the difference between us?*

But I don't say anything.

I just smile back.

And walk away.

The walk is over quickly—too quickly. The wide avenues turn into the small canals and streets around the center of Amsterdam. And then I'm there. I'm at the warehouse—263 Prinsengracht. I stare at the wide, wooden warehouse doors and at the narrow door up the steps that I'm meant to go through.

I'm scared.

I want to run. I want to run and run and never stop until I find Liese. I'll hold her hand, and we'll run together until we find some woods, some hills, some caves to hide in. But there aren't any—only flatlands. We've already fled from Germany to here. And now we're surrounded. The Nazis are everywhere: Luxembourg, Belgium, France. Holland is just a small pocket in a whole coat made of Nazis. There is nowhere else for us to run. I stare at the doors.

I feel sick.

I feel the sun hot on my back.

I turn and look down the street. I shouldn't be doing this, I shouldn't be doing anything that draws attention to me—but I can't help it. I turn and look down the long, narrow street. I look at the trees and the water of the canal. I look at the people walking past me, but it doesn't matter now how long I stand here, looking. Nothing will change.

Liese's not coming back.

I'm probably never going to see her again.

———

My name is Peter van Pels. I'm nearly sixteen years old. I walk up the stone steps and turn the handle of the narrow wooden door. I push it open and step forward. The door closes itself behind me.

I can still see the street and feel the soft, summer air.
Fresh air. In the Annex I remembered air the way I
now remember the taste of fresh vegetables and the
sound of laughter.

As something already lost—and best forgotten.

JULY 13, 1942 — PETER ENTERS THE ANNEX:
PRINSENGRACHT, AMSTERDAM

It's dark and hot between the two doors. The air is stale. I push on through the second door and up the stairway. I picture the diagram of the house in my mind.

I must get it right. I must be quiet. I walk past a window with OFFICE written on it. There are voices behind it, shadows of people moving. I'm a ghost; they don't know I'm here. I move quietly along the dark, narrow corridor. The heat is stifling. Up some more stairs and the corridor widens. On my left is a window, covered in dark fabric. Below it another staircase going down. It's dark. I stand and wait for my eyes to adjust. In front of me is a wide door with a latch on it. I don't want to go through it. I want to turn back. I want to run. And then in my mind I see the van disappearing down the street. My heart's beating so fast I can't breathe. I lift the latch quickly, before I can think, and open the door.

I hear a voice high and clear:

"Well, we're lucky, aren't we? Imagine if we didn't have a father to find us an annex, or if we were all stuck in here hating each other!"

I feel a sharp stab of irritation. Anne Frank, as loud and sure of herself as ever!

Lucky? How can we be lucky? She makes it sound as though we're playing a parlor game.

Straight in front of me is another staircase, steep and dangerous. To the left is where the voices are. Everything is small and cramped like the streets and canals outside. And dark.

I turn left and stand in the doorway. The Franks are sitting at a table. They all turn and stare at me.

"Oh!" says Mrs. Frank. For a moment there's a shocked silence. We all stare at each other. "Oh, Peter! It's you! For a moment I didn't recognize you."

I blink. It's hard to see their faces clearly in the half-light. Mr. Frank is standing up and walking toward me. He smiles. "Peter. You're here. Let me show you your room."

"Room!" says Anne. "That's not what I'd call it!"

"Anne!" says her mother. I don't look at her. Anne Frank thinks enough of herself already, without me joining in.

"Hello, Peter," says Margot, quietly. *Why are you here?* The thought flashes furiously across my mind—*Why are you here, and not Liese!* I nod at her.

Mr. Frank takes me back to the steep stairs. I follow him up, slowly. We go through a kitchen.

"This will be your parents' room and our communal kitchen. We all have to double up, I'm afraid."

I don't say anything. I can't. Next to the sink is a doorway. He steps through it.

"And this is *your* bedroom."

There is a window, covered with a dark blind. It's hard to believe the sun is still out there behind it—shining. We're pushed up close together by the lack of space. Beside us is another staircase going up.

"Above you are the attics, where we store everything, and hang washing—that means you'll have us all traipsing through here, I'm afraid."

At least there's light coming from somewhere.

"The attic windows are too high to be covered," says Mr. Frank, "and so at least this room has some light!" As though he can read my mind. I take a deep breath. Squashed up next to the staircase is a bed. At the bottom of the bed is a desk.

"Well," he says, "it's perhaps not what we'd normally call a room, but it's all yours."

I sit down on the bed.

"Thank you," I say. The words come out small.

"I'll leave you then . . ." But he stops at the door. "Would you like to see the bathroom?"

I shake my head.

"You know the names of all the office workers downstairs who'll be helping us, don't you?"

I shake my head, I can't remember. Mr. Frank smiles.

"Well, you'll have plenty of time to get to know them. There's Miep Gies—she's our main contact with the outside world—then there's Mr. Kugler, Mr. Kleiman, and Bep and her father, Mr. Voskuijl."

"Thank you," I say again.

"Well, come downstairs and have a drink when you're ready—and welcome, Peter!"

"Thank you," I say quickly. I want him to go away.

I lie down. I close my eyes. Behind them the heat throbs in my head. The room is airless. If I stretch out my arms . . . if I stretch out my arms they'll crash into the walls on one side and the staircase on the other. If I stretch out my legs, my feet will hit the door. I lie on the bed and keep everything close to my sides. Somewhere outside, the church clock rings the quarter hour.

I close my eyes and begin to shake. I open them, but I can still see Liese's face at the window—and the van disappearing.

Where is she?

Where will they take her?

The sound of voices next door wakes me.

"Mrs. van Pels, have you really brought hats in your hat-box?" laughs Anne.

"No! No!" says Mother. "It's not a hat in there, it's a . . . chamber pot!"

They all laugh, Mutti loudest of all. I pull the sheet up over me. I hide my head beneath its light cotton and curl up, trying to escape, but the picture keeps on coming . . . Liese's face . . . A bright hot pain sears through my head. White, like lightning.

Mutti steps through the doorway. "Peter?" she asks. "Peter!" She reaches for my hand but I put it quickly under the sheet. She bites her lip.

"You're here!" she says. "Thank God!"

"Why wouldn't I be?"

She stares at me. I look away.

So she knew.

She sensed that I wanted to run.

I don't say anything.

I want her to go away.

But she doesn't, she looks around instead.

"Oh, Petel!" she whispers. "It's so small." And then she takes a deep breath. "But at least we're all here. And we're all safe!"

Except Liese.

I don't say anything. I don't ever say anything much anyway, unlike the Franks—but I think a lot. I wonder how this can be called living. How can we be in a space this small? We're trapped in this building like rats in a sinking ship, waiting to be caught. The pain flashes through my head again, lightning striking a steeple.

Anne's voice floats up the stairs: "We've made tons and tons of jam already . . . and doesn't the whole place smell wonderful—of cherries and sugar! Oh, and Daddy, I think this must be the best hiding place in the whole of Holland!"

I feel my body tighten. I can't help it, or do anything about it. It flinches at her words. It's taking on a life of its own. It's like it's trying to crawl away through the walls, back to the outside.

Back to wherever Liese is.

Why didn't I stay? Why didn't I fight? Why did I stand there with a stone in my hand doing nothing?

I groan out loud.

"She makes it sound like we're at a tea party!" I hiss.

"Peter!" says Mutti. "We must be—"

"Grateful," I say quickly, because if I hear *her* say it I think I might have to scream or slap her.

Mutti stares at me. "I'm sorry," she says. "I know it'll be hard for you, but we are lucky. Lucky to be alive and lucky to have someone prepared to help hide us!"

Lucky! That word again. Lucky!

I don't feel lucky.

"Peter?" she asks, and I turn to look at her.

"What?"

"There wasn't only a chamber pot in that box, you know!"

She gestures to the door. Standing on the threshold, head cocked to one side and ears erect, is Mouschi. My cat.

"Oh!" I say. Mutti smiles.

Mouschi leaps up onto my bed and curls into my side.

"Thank you!" I say.

"Well, now that he's here, what can anyone say?" she whispers.

I don't answer; I just bury my head in his fur. When I look up, she's gone.

I didn't know.

I didn't know that a bed below an attic is a luxury. I didn't know that to grieve, as I was grieving for my freedom, is a blessing and a privilege, as well as a sorrow.

Here in the lager there are no feelings. Only the minutes passing, the one foot in front of the other, the mud, the staying upright, the hanging on to the spoon for your soup so that no one steals it. You cannot grieve for another. You are too busy making sure that it will not be you.

AUGUST 8, 1942 — PETER IS HAUNTED BY LIESE IN HIS DREAMS

I wake up, my heart beating fast, clicking along like a train through a tunnel. Darkness.

Wetness in my hands.

Eyes wide open and searching through the dark.

I'm trying to hold on to something. My mind gropes for it, but it's gone. It's over. Limp and finished. I feel my face flush red in the night. I listen. Somewhere in the distance the church clock strikes three. Next door, Mutti groans and turns over.

Did I make a sound? Did anyone hear me?

I listen to the silence. It's so high up here. The whole night feels different.

The memory of the dream comes without warning. I dreamed of Liese. Liese in a crowd. She is carried along by a river of people. Her dark hair a dot among many.

"Liese!"

I scream her name.

I'm terrified that no one knows who she is. No one but me.

She turns. Her violet eyes are wide and frightened. Our

eyes catch before she's carried away by the stream of people. Forced along by the high banks of soldiers beside them.

Suddenly I'm right up next to her. Pressed against her by the thousands of bodies around us. They lift us up from the ground. I feel my face sink into her breasts, my arms lock around her body. I feel us carried along as her legs surround my waist . . . I bury myself in her. I hold on tight until we explode together.

And then I'm far away above us both, watching the memories pour out of me. The taste of her lips, the feel of her skin beneath my fingers, the first time I saw her, her hands moving across the piano keys, the day I asked to carry her books . . . the memories fall around us like rain as we cling together.

But the river of people keeps on moving—as though nothing is happening at all.

"Liese," I whisper.

She holds my face in her hands and we stare into each other's eyes.

"Peter!"

I reach out but she's already beyond me. I watch, helpless, as she disappears into the crowd. Calling my name. "Peter!"

I am Peter—the thought wakes me.

This is who I am.

I am Peter.

I whisper the words into the night.

I try to hold on to the remembered warmth of Liese's body in the sheets.

I don't know how I am to wash the sheets. I don't know how I am to hide my shame. I don't know how I am to live anymore.

Yes, I am Peter—but will somebody tell me how?

AUGUST 9, 1942 — PETER IS SUFFOCATING IN THE ANNEX

"Petel! Petel!" Mother's voice wakes me. "Get up. Everybody is wondering where you are!"

But I can't. It's always so dark in here, it's like the day never really begins. I wake up so tired.

"I'm tired," I say. I turn over.

"You've got five minutes!" she hisses. She's embarrassed by me. I should be awake and not asleep. I should feel lucky and not worried that I might be dying. But all I want to do is sleep.

The kitchen is right next door to my room. Everyone has breakfast there. I can hear everything. Father's telling everyone how cleverly he fooled people into thinking that the Franks had fled to Maastricht. I stumble into the room. Nobody greets me they just glance at me, at my slept-in clothes and my filthy hair. I sit down. They nod at me and carry on.

I wonder if I'm really here.

The story is "What Happened When the Franks Left." I've heard it a million times already, we all have, but they still go on and on. I try to listen to the words, but the sound of their voices comes at me from a long way away. The words all make sense in my head, but I keep on getting the feelings wrong. I shiver, when everyone else is laughing.

Anne looks at me—a harsh, questioning look. A slow blush crawls over my cheeks. She looks away, scornful.

"... and old Mrs. Siedle told me herself that she had seen you all loaded into a military vehicle!" says Mutti.

I remember the feel of my foot hitting Liese's garden wall. I hear the military engine coming down the street.

"Yes!" laughs Papi, taking over. "I heard it myself, too! And here we are, sitting right in the middle of the same city! Who would believe it?"

They all laugh. Anne glances at me again, sharp: "Peter doesn't think it's funny," she says.

I stand up too quickly and the chair falls over. Slowly their eyes land on me. I try to stand up straight and be polite. I don't know what's happening to me. My head's full of shavings—leftover pieces with no shape or meaning. "Excuse me," I say, and feel my face blush. I leave the room. Behind me I hear Anne clap her hands like a child with a new present.

"Now no one will *ever* guess. Ever!" The laughter goes on.

I don't lie down on my bed, I drop down. I fall away from the thoughts that won't stop churning inside me.

Where are you, Liese?

How can this be funny?

Am I the only person in the world not laughing?

Falling asleep feels wrong—it feels like drowning.

———

I can't get up. The days go by—half-light, half-dark. I sleep. I eat, but the food doesn't taste of anything. I blush and stumble when the Franks talk to me.

I dream of Liese. And sometimes I wake with my sheets wet and my heart wild. I'm not sure what's real anymore. I think Anne came and stood in my doorway.

"Do you like your room, Peter?"

"It's not a room, it's a corridor." She raises her eyes to the ceiling. She's so thin, a child really, not like Liese.

Liese.

Liese.

Liese.

Where are you? What's happening to you? I shiver. When I look up, Anne's gone. I'm not sure she was ever there.

———

If I close my eyes I can feel Liese's hands landing on me. Light. Soft, like butterflies. I nearly groan aloud. Stifle it. I feel a pain like longing, an ache in my side. I can't breathe.

Am I dying? I think I must be.

"I'm dying!" I can't believe I've really said the words aloud, but I must have, because everyone's looking at me.

I blush.

"Honestly, Peter!" Mrs. Frank says as she flicks out a clean tea towel.

"Have you ever heard of the word *hypochondria?*" asks Anne.

"I can't breathe!" I whisper.

"Perhaps if you did a bit more and slept a bit less?" Mr. Frank says gently.

Mutti and Papi look furiously at each other.

No one believes I'm ill.

I go back to bed.

The Westertoren church bells strike midnight. I creep up the attic steps. One of the windows is very slightly open. I lie down and breathe in the fresh, outside air. Gulp it.

"Can you hear the bells, Liese?"

I look at the moon, the way we always promised each other we would. We never said goodbye, just:

"At ten."

"At ten."

I whisper the words—is she doing the same some-where?

Where are you?

I fall asleep in the wisp of air from the window. I don't

dream. I sleep wondering if the moon is shining down on us both. All through the night I hear the church bells striking through my dreams.

Can you hear them, Liese?

When I wake up, it's light. Birds are singing in the big chestnut tree outside. My neck is stiff and my head hangs sideways off my neck like it's cocked and listening. Or broken. Listening for something no longer there.

The clock chimes five times. I hear it again, beneath the bells, the click of wheels against the track, the trains that carry us all away. Where to? There are whispers like wheels. Rumors like dark tunnels. But we know really, don't we? We all know, but we can't say it.

Camps.

Death camps.

Suddenly I know it, feel it. She's gone. She was here in Amsterdam, where she could hear the clock, but now she's gone—into that river of people.

I crawl, stiff and slow, down the attic steps.

"Peter!"

Mutti stands at the bottom of the steps, staring up at me. How long has she been there?

"What?" I begin, and then I see my filthy sheet rolled up in her hand. On my bed is a clean, white flat sheet. We glance at each other, look away.

"I . . ."

"Shh!" she smiles at me. "Don't worry. I can wash it before the Franks are even up, and we can replace their sheet. They won't notice."

"Thanks," I mutter, but she's already gone.

The bed feels good. Cool and clean. I sleep without dreams.

When I wake up again, breakfast is over.

When I dream of Mutti, that's how I see her, standing at the bottom of the stairs. The way she did when I was a child, her legs braced and arms raised, waiting for me to leap into her arms.

I dream I'm in clean sheets on a real mattress, and that I'll wake with the sun on my face. Best of all, I'll turn, and go back to sleep in the sunlight.

But it's only a dream.

When I wake, I crawl over all the dead and dying bodies to piss in the pot. I listen. Good the pot is not too full. To piss when it's full can mean death. You have to go out into the freezing night and empty it. After that all sleep is over.

All hope of rest is gone.

I crawl back and wait for the word that drags us from our bunks:

WYSTAWACH.

Wake up.

But it doesn't come.

AUGUST 21, 1942 — PETER'S FATHER IS ANGRY

"Peter! Peter! Peter!"

I didn't know I was asleep. My name comes at me, hissing and angry.

"Peter! Peter! Peter!" It's Father, calling me. I sit bolt upright.

"What?" I'm about to shout, but his hand covers my mouth quickly, forcing my head back down onto the pillow.

"It's only me: Papi," he hisses. "It's OK, don't make a sound."

I force my body to go limp. I close my eyes. I feel my heart beating.

"Get up," he hisses. "Get up and help. Right now. Do you hear me?"

I don't answer. I try to take his hand away without opening my eyes, but he keeps it there.

"You could at least try to be a man!" he says. I turn over. I want to go back to sleep, to be anywhere but here.

"How dare you shame us all like this!" he hisses. "You're nearly sixteen years old. Get up. Stand up. Start helping. Those two girls do more than you." He takes his hand away.

"If I can't fight, what point is there?" I don't know where

29

the words come from; they are just there, between us. The shock of them makes me open my eyes. We stare at each other.

"Fight!" he says, and he sits back and shakes his head at me. "You think you can fight this? Get up and make yourself useful, that's how we fight."

I don't move. I try not to blink. I stare at him.

"Show me you can get out of bed and do a day's work before you talk of fighting!" he says.

"You're in my way," I hiss back. He stands up. I run my hands through my hair, it's stiff with dirt. I get up slowly, partly because I'm still shaking, partly just to annoy him. He stands by the attic steps. There's not enough room to change with him there. I can't get up without having to touch him.

"I'll see you in the kitchen," he says. "Two minutes."

I don't say anything. I wait for him to leave, and then I dress.

I go downstairs. Mr. Kugler is trying to make the entrance to the Annex secret.

"Hello," he says. He has a nice face. "Can you give me a hand?"

I try. I collect wood shavings and put them in a pillow-case. I make a pad for the door to stop everyone from banging their heads on the frame. It's awkward and useless work, ugly, not like the things I used to make for Aunt Henny:

mending the pieces she loved, fixing her sofa. I need to forget about all that. We've disguised the door as a bookcase, and the lintel is hidden, so you have to duck down. *Great, I think, a bookcase. As though it isn't bad enough already being locked up with the book-crazy Franks.*

"Oh!" says Anne. "So you've graced us with your presence, have you?" I don't answer. I'd like to. I'd like to ask her why she's always breaking things, dropping them, and banging into things? Why isn't she more careful? Why does she always behave as though this is a house party?

But I don't say anything.

"Thank you, Peter," says Margot.

"That's all right." I blush. Margot turns away, trying not to see, but Anne stares at me as though she is trying to decide exactly what shade of red I'm going. I turn away and stumble back upstairs.

"What an idiot!" says Anne, and then she drops her cup and they both start laughing.

Mutti's at the door to my room, smiling at me like I've just wiped out a whole platoon of Nazis all by myself, not simply nailed up a bag full of wood shavings!

"Better?" she asks.

"Better," I say, even though it isn't.

"Unlike your hair!" And she smiles. I smile back. It feels strange, muscles creaking into a new shape.

"Let me wash it for you," she says, and I'm about to say no, but then I think of her stealing an extra sheet out of the communal cupboard. I think of the clean white sheet on my bed. I think of how she washes away my sins and dries them—all without saying a word. I think of the insults she takes from Mrs. Frank because of me.

"If you think you can use all of our sheets and none of your own you are very much mistaken!" says Mrs. Frank. Mutti says nothing, nothing of how they use our bowls and hide their own. Of how Anne has broken nearly all of ours and never said sorry. So I say yes. I let her wash my filthy hair.

She scrubs and digs and rubs at my scalp as though she could chase all the evil away with her fingers. It hurts. At last she is done.

"Ah!" she says. "Now you are my Petel."

"Thanks," I mutter.

"Margot!" We both hear Anne's voice outside the bathroom door. "His mother's in there washing his hair! I'm only thirteen and I even dye my own mustache!"

"Shhh!" says Margot quickly, but the damage is done. Mutti's smile falls off her face and all the way to the floor. Poor old Mutti; never as good as the Franks, never as clever, or funny—or wise. If Anne were a boy I'd punch her. I'd spit on my palms, draw a line straight between those brown superior eyes and land my fist right in the middle of all that confidence.

I hate her.

"Much better," I say out loud. "Thank you, Mutti, I feel wonderful."

And as soon as I say it, I realize it's true.

I do feel better.

A bit.

Anne and Margot have discovered the attic. It's a pain. The way they just walk right through my "room" to get to it. I know. I know. The world is ending outside the Annex (as Anne calls it) or at least it is for the Jews and gypsies and anyone else who doesn't measure up to the Nazi standard! Mr. Frank said they think they know we're Jewish by measuring our noses, or our skulls! Mutti snorted and said, "Well, I know an easier way to tell if a man's a Jew!" But she didn't say it in front of the Franks; she waited until it was just the three of us alone, upstairs.

All that happening outside, and I'm stupid enough to be angry with two of the most annoying girls in the world. At least Margot looks a bit apologetic, but Anne! She just flounces through my room.

"Any ailments today, Petel-pie?" she laughs.

They spend ages up there, taking it for themselves, the only place where we can see the sky.

Mrs. Frank does try to cut Anne down to size: "Hanneli's mother was right about you, Anne," she says. "Do you remember what she said?"

Anne glares at her mother, then turns to her father who looks away. I think he might be smiling.

34

"She said, 'God knows everything, but Anne Frank always knows it better.' Well, you don't know it better, young lady!" says Mrs. Frank.

Anne goes white with rage and her lips tremble. She storms off, saying nothing.

We all pretend to be busy. After a while Margot follows her.

"Well!" says Mrs. Frank. "No doubt that's another episode for Kitty to enjoy." Mr. Frank glances at her—a warning glance. I wonder who Kitty is, and how Anne keeps in touch with her.

"Every child needs privacy. What she writes in her diary is her business," remarks her father in his normal voice, quiet and calm. No one has heard Mr. Frank raise his voice. Ever.

"But why call her diary Kitty?" asks Mrs. Frank. But Mr. Frank doesn't answer, just shakes his paper.

Ah! So Anne keeps a diary. I bet I know what she writes in it—how wonderful she is!

AUGUST 26, 1942 — PETER DISCOVERS THE JOYS OF READING

During the day, all the office workers are downstairs: Miep, Bep, Mr. Kugler, Mr. Kleiman—and so on. We are entirely dependent on them. They bring us our food. They order the courses for Anne and Margot to study. They drop off Anne's magazines and they give us paper. They do everything for us.

All we do is sit here.

Today Miep brought yet more books—a great pile of them on the table. We're meant to study. That's easy for Anne and Margot because they *want* to study Greek and Latin and so on and so on . . . but I don't. I want to make things, to be a carpenter. There are no books for that. But there on the table *is* a book I would like to read, even though I know Papi wouldn't want me to. Just seeing its cover makes me think of Liese. I want it. I pick it up and glance at it. No one notices, or says anything.

"He held her in his arms, her breath came faster as his lips brushed her . . ." I look up and carefully, casually, I drop it back on the pile—then I pick up an armful of books and walk away. Nobody says anything, only Mutti glances at me,

a smile at the corners of her mouth. Our eyes hold for a second and I know she won't say anything.

"Anything good?" asks Mr. Frank from behind his newspaper.

"Oh! I like a good romance myself," Mutti says loudly. "The best type is where the hero is very tall, very dark, and very bad . . . a bit like you, perhaps, Otto!"

Mr. Frank's eyes open wide. "I hardly think I'm the type of man who . . . Oh, Gusti," he says, "you're teasing me!" And he smiles, raising his newspaper. The other Franks all look at Mutti as though she is slightly mad, but she doesn't care. She's covering for me. Only Anne answers her. "Oh yes!" she breathes at Mutti, her hands clasped beneath her chin. "There's nothing like a good story!"

I'm in the attic. The sun shines and I sit in it and read. The book makes time change. Stops it hanging. Somewhere I can hear the breeze in the tree behind me. I can feel the sun on my back and the pages turn and I forget. There are only the people on the page and what will happen next. What will happen to the people in the book, not what will happen to me—or what might be happening to Liese. I forget everything. I even forget the time—until I hear Papi behind me.

"Peter!"

He's standing at the top of the stairs. Of course he is. We can't shout anymore. We can't bang doors or run upstairs, or storm outside if we're angry. We sneak up on each other and hiss instead of shout.

"Peter, come down! What have you been do—" And then he sees the book in my hands. He doesn't say anything at all, or give me a chance to explain, he just grabs it from my hands and turns away from me, walking quickly down the stairs. For a moment I'm so startled I just sit there, but then I stand up and follow. I want that book. I want to know what happens.

Everyone's in the kitchen, it must be lunchtime. I don't care. I grab the book out of his hands. He grabs it back. We struggle. I'm winning. I realize I am bigger and stronger than him and that I will . . . and then he SMACKS me!

I drop the book. I drop it so I can hit him. I draw my fist back and . . . *I can't do it. I can't do it.* The thoughts fly through my head as my fist waits. What if I hurt him? What if he needs a doctor? Where will we get one? I turn and run from the room. I can't even hit my own father, what use would I be to any resistance?

I run to the attic. My heart is wild. My guts are writhing . . . I don't know what to do. I walk up and down. I throw open the window, I don't care who sees it. I wonder if I can make it across the roofs. I have to get out, but the window won't open wide enough to let me through. I'm trapped.

I want to . . .

I want to . . .

SCREAM.

I want to stretch out my arms and knock the walls down. I want to run so far and fast that I remember what it's like to feel my breath burn in my body. I want to move. I want to live. I want to . . .

I whistle. I whistle so loud that I imagine the whole of Holland could hear me. I'm a Jew. I'm a Jew! And I'm right here in the middle of Amsterdam. Hiding. Hear me! I take a big, deep breath and shout as loud as I can down the chimney.

"I won't come down . . . *down* . . . *down!*" My voice echoes through the pipe and out into the rooms below.

I start to laugh

Out loud.

There! At last! A *real* silence in the Annex. Not the silence that hangs around us all the time and that we're so afraid to break, but a proper silence. I made it. I imagine them all sitting down there with their breath held, waiting . . .

Waiting . . .

Waiting, to know if my scream has made anybody in the houses and gardens around us jump, look up, and reach for the telephone . . .

But all that happens is that Papi shouts too.

"I've had enough of that boy!"

I've made him shout! I've made him shout as loud as me. They appear at the top of the stairs. Him and Mr. Frank.

"Apologize!" says Father.

"Peter, you should go to your room and think about this," says Mr. Frank.

I stand very still. The truth is I'm so afraid of what I've done, I *can't* move. "Peter?" asks Mr. Frank.

They begin to walk toward me. I back away until I can feel the wall behind me and there's nowhere else to go. They stretch out their hands toward me. They're taking me back down, back into the dark and the whispers and the dreams. I push them away. I kick and scream and twist and turn like the pain and fear in my guts, but they hold me tight. They lift me down the stairs and drop me on the bed.

I turn to the wall.

"One day, Peter, and hopefully it will be soon, you'll learn to think of others instead of yourself," says Father.

"Try to understand," says Mr. Frank. "And please, Peter, no more noise. That's important."

They leave.

My fingers reach out and touch the wall.

My face is wet.

I think I must be crying.

AUGUST 28, 1942, EVENING — PETER
WAKES UP IN HIS ROOM

When I wake there are voices in the kitchen and the light from the attic is fading. I go up the stairs and stand by the window. I look at the outside. I watch as the light fades right out of the sky, and is gone.

Outside.

Outside.

How can one small word mean such a big thing?

I watch as the branches of the chestnut tree slowly darken and turn black against the sky. The wind drops. The leaves are still. The sun fades and dips beyond the square of the window. The clouds are lit up with gold in the middle; deep dark lines score their edges. I watch the color leave them, watch it leak out in pink and purple, until the whole sky is burning and bruised and finally black.

I watch the night come, and the day end. I understand that I am saying goodbye. Not just to this day itself, but to the world outside.

Outside.

I'm giving it up.

I have to because there's no place for me in it. If I can't give it up then I put us all in danger. I know that now.

The clock strikes half past midnight. Outside there are no stars in our patch of sky. I stand up in the dark. I feel stiff and grope my way to the top of the steep stairs. For a moment I stand still. I listen to my breathing in the dark.

I'm scared.

Scared that I might fall and never stop.

Scared that I'll never make love to a girl.

Scared I'm a coward.

Scared we're trapped.

Scared we'll be caught.

Scared that it's my own ghost standing there, waiting for me at the bottom of the stairs. That this is it—all that's left of my life.

I take a step forward . . . first one and then another . . . I feel my way in the dark, until I'm at the bottom of the stairs and can reach out in the dark for the edge of my bed.

I lie in it with my eyes wide open—and wait for sleep.

SEPTEMBER 15, 1942 — ANNE AND PETER ARGUE

Anne's standing in my doorway. For once she's not insulting me. She just insults my room instead.

"You know, Peter, if only you put a rug there and a cupboard on the wall, or maybe some pictures . . . Mmm!" she says, and she puts one hand on her hip and her head to one side, a finger on her lips. She's looking at my tiny room, but by the look in her eyes it could be a palace—with her, of course, as its world-class decorator. She makes me smile sometimes, even though she's so irritating, especially when she comes into my room without asking.

"Mmm," she says again, "you could put up a table or a shelf and do you have your own bedcover? Patchwork is good to brighten a dark room, and there's space on your wall for pictures . . ." She casts me a sly glance, as if she knows exactly who I'd like to hang on my wall. And she goes on talking. I stare at her. The words don't stop. They just pour out of her. If they were bullets, we could stop a whole platoon with them. A few thousand Annes and the world might be saved. I see a picture in my mind, a cartoon. A frontline full of Annes.

"Talk!" yells the commanding officer and at once they all begin. The opposition fall like skittles as the words hit them.

I laugh. Then blush. Anne stops mid-sentence. We stare at each other. She's very thin. Her eyes are very brown and the light in them dances. Her hair curls and kinks around her face like electricity. But behind all her words she's still a child—not like Liese.

"What was in the book you stole?" she blurts out. I blush again.

"It's not for children," I say.

She curls her lip and turns on her heel. She changes her mind, stops and looks back at me. She's angry, there are two bright spots of red on her cheeks.

"It's obvious to everyone, you know," she says.

"What is?" I ask. I feel the blush hot on my cheeks, and my heart sinks.

"That you're a lovesick puppy!" she hisses, and she spins around and leaves.

Hearing her say it, it's like a punch in the gut. Is it? Is it obvious? I hate her. What does she know? Nothing but books and words. I'm furious. I'm blushing and that just makes me even more furious. What right does she have to come into my room? Who does she think she is? Mutti says we should put a pea in her bed and see if she's really quite as noble as she thinks she is.

A lovesick puppy!

The words tear at me.

Am I lovesick?

Yes. I think I am.

Is it something to be ashamed of?

I don't know.

Maybe sometimes there are no answers. Maybe sometimes there are only the feelings and the questions—like, where are you, Liese?

Are you dead?

Why?

Because you were born a Jew.

Why?

Another question no one can answer.

Maybe I'm ashamed because it's hard *not* to feel ashamed, when just being born is something you can be killed for.

I remember that feeling, that shame. But shame is a feeling for free men. I am less than a man now. I am a Häftling—a beast of burden, carrying their hate. A beast who has been forced to lose sight of everything except the effort of putting one foot in front of the other. And when that fails, I must take one breath after the other—and survive.

Lying here doing nothing makes the feelings waken.

I do not want to feel.

This shame—the shame of being a Häftling.

SEPTEMBER 23, 1942 — ANNE AND PETER ARE PLAYING IN THE ATTIC

Nothing happens. Everything happens. Anne reads and talks and drives us all mad. Margot studies and cleans and is kind and quiet. Mutti cooks and flirts with Mr. Frank (yes she does, I know she does, I wish she wouldn't, but maybe she's bored, like I am). Papi looks forward to the next meal, repairs everything until there's nothing left that's broken—and smokes and tells jokes. Mrs. Frank mends our clothes, praises Margot, and gets angry with Anne. Mr. Frank reads and smiles and tries to keep the peace. Some nights we listen to the radio. I hate it. It reminds me that everyone's fighting while I just sit here—and listen.

Afterward we all argue about what it means.

"You see it will all be over in a few months!"

"It will never end and we'll all die in the camps!"

But all we're really talking about is how we feel that day. Yet you must never say so—*ever!* If you do you are suddenly the enemy, and you'll be shot down in flames, like a plane.

We don't want reason. We don't want truth. We just want to believe that the British will come, because if they don't . . . well if they don't, we won't be here to tell anyone about it.

Which is why . . . we don't want reason and we don't want truth. We just want to believe . . . and so we go on. Round and round, in the same rooms, with the same people. In the half-dark. It's always half dark, even in the daytime. Only in the attic is there light. And sky. But in winter I know that some days the light will never arrive. The thought scares me.

Anne appears in my room and asks, "Do you like dressing up?"

I nod. And blush again. I think she means wearing nice clothes to go out in, but she doesn't, she means dressing up like children out of a dressing-up box.

"Come on!" she says, and her eyes are shining the way no one's eyes shine anymore, not even Margot's. And I'm *bored*. Nothing ever happens and we're supposed to be *glad* about it. Well, the truth is that we *are* glad about it, because we're so scared about what *could* happen—which might explain why I'm creeping down the attic staircase with Mutti's dress pinched between my finger and thumb, hoping that I don't fall down the stairs and end up needing a doctor. Anne is behind me wearing her father's hat and a penciled mustache. My God, if my friend Hans could see me now! I can't even bear to think about it. Anne runs into the kitchen.

"Please put your hands together for . . ."

I don't know what to do. I start to sweat. Anne's hissing at me: "Come on!"

I walk into the kitchen and see Mutti, smiling. Without thinking, I twitch my skirt and turn my head over my shoulder, just the way she does sometimes.

Anne picks up a book and coughs, just like her father, and begins telling me in terrible Dutch (all our parents speak bad Dutch—they make it sound like German!) all about Descartes. She sounds just like Mr. Frank! I act like Mutti, trying to look like I understand what she's saying, nodding my head. I cuddle up close to Anne and peer at the book, asking more and more stupid questions. Every time she answers, she steps away from me and I step closer. She stares, her eyes wide in mock alarm (just like her father).

I step so close I breathe into her neck, so close I can smell her. She smells of the soap we all use, and something else . . . something that's just her.

Just Anne.

And then Margot laughs out loud and I step away. We bow deeply, doff our hats and run out. We're laughing so much we have to help each other up the attic steps.

"Oh, that's a tonic!" I hear Mutti laugh. "Am I really quite so obvious?"

"Auguste, you're charming!" says Mr. Frank.

I can't get the dress off. It's stuck halfway! My rear's out one end and my head's lost inside it.

"Breathe out!" says Anne and she pulls. I go one way,

and Anne and the dress go the other. We lie on the floor, laughing.

"Look!" says Anne. "Look up!"

And I look up. In our patch of sky a thousand stars are glittering.

"Amazing!" I say.

OCTOBER 8, 1942 — MIEP MAKES A
DIFFICULT DECISION

Miep is crying. She sits in the kitchen. We watch as the tears roll down her face. We all stare at her. We don't know what to do. What can we do? Our lives are in the hands she holds up to her face. She thinks she should be able to save everyone, but today she had to make a choice—and she chose us. We're grateful, but we're sad, too—and ashamed. At least I am, that Miep had to make this choice.

An old woman, or us.

The Gestapo left an old Jewish woman outside Miep's house to wait for transport. She banged and banged on the door and when Miep finally opened it, the woman begged Miep to save her, to take her in. But how could she? The police knew the woman was there. If Miep let her in, they might arrest her or search her workplace. And then what would they find? Us.

And so now Miep sits at the kitchen table. Crying.

"But that poor woman, what'll become of her?" she says, and the tears flow again. We don't cry. Are we all thinking the same thing—that it could be us next time? Sometime. Anytime. A different knock at the door. We don't want to answer Miep. We can't. We don't want to think about what might become of the old lady, because it means thinking about what might become of us. Miep notices, like she notices everything.

"I'm being silly. Honestly! Anyone would think it was me in danger."

She straightens her back and says to Mutti, "I don't ever want anyone to find you, Auguste, you make the best soup in the whole of Holland!"

Mutti smiles. "For the best woman in the whole of Holland!" she says, and we all agree. That's exactly what Miep is—and the rest of them in the office—all of them are in danger, risking their lives just for us.

As she leaves, Mr. Frank puts his hand on her shoulder.

"It's not you who made this evil, Miep, but it *is* you fighting it. We're grateful."

She smiles at him. "Thank you!" she says.

But he shrugs. "No, it's us who should thank you," and he smiles back. I can see she feels better.

He's like that, Mr. Frank.

Yes. Yes he is. He was.

If I believed in any of it I'd say he had God in his soul, but I don't believe. Not anymore. I think Mr. Frank had something better than God, something they couldn't touch or fight or gas. Something they couldn't destroy—not in him anyway. He had hope—and a belief.

That most of us are good.

I'm glad I helped keep him alive, right up until the end at Auschwitz.

Until I . . .

LATER THAT DAY

After lunch I go and stand in the attic and look at the sky.

There are still so many questions inside me. Why do they help us—Miep and Bep and Mr. Kleiman and Kugler? I try to ask them, but they shush me—as though I were still a child. They tell me that the Dutch hate the Nazis and that if they have to, they'll fight them until the whole of Holland is empty and silent.

Amsterdam empty . . . I imagine it: just the trees lining the canals—looking down at themselves in the water—drifting leaves, empty boats. The gulls. I get out my pencil and begin to draw. When the picture's finished I feel better.

I hear footsteps on the stairs and hide my drawing quickly. Mr. Frank appears.

"All right?" he asks.

"Why should they go on protecting us?" I blurt out.

Mr. Frank stares at me for a long time before he answers "Well, partly because we pay their wages."

"But how could you say that?"

"Because it's *one* of the reasons, Peter. A minor one, but important not to forget. Mostly they do it because they feel that what's happening is wrong, and they want no part of it. More than that, they want to stop it."

"But it doesn't affect them, they're not Jewish, are they?"

He sighs. "It's not just about Jews, Peter, is it? It's about all the people the Nazis hate. I think the office workers know that it *does* affect them, Peter—that's what makes them so special. What's happening to us is about everyone, although they blame us first, last, and most of all. It's about hate. We can't stand by and do nothing when people are killed for their difference."

I take a deep breath. "But we *are* doing nothing. Why aren't we fighting?" He steps back, and I realize I hissed it out at him. I blush again. I didn't mean to.

"We're doing *our* job, Peter. They're doing *theirs*. Does the chick put its head out of the nest while its mother fights the kestrel?"

"What?"

But he doesn't answer. He's looking out at the sky, over the rooftops at the horizon and all the way to the sea. He's looking at it like he wonders sometimes, too, if it's all really still there.

"They're full of hate, Peter! So full of it that they turn it into hating us—into hating anything that's different—and then they try to kill it. They're trying to wipe us out: country by country, city by city, like pestilence. But one day, someday, maybe even after we've all gone, they'll have to look at themselves—and the hate will still be there. What then? I wonder. But until then . . ." He breathes out. Shakes his head. "This is nothing new. Our job is not to fight, not now. Our job is to survive it. Especially the young. Especially you. How else will the world know what's happened? If youth goes, where is our future?"

I step back. I've never heard him rant like this. He's a bit frightening.

"Stay alive. That's your job, Peter. There will be others out there, fighting."

"Jews?" I ask.

He smiles. "Of course!" he says. "What? Do you think there are none of us resisting?"

"I don't know," I whisper.

"Well, even by the law of averages it's probable that there are, wouldn't you say?"

I shrug. "I don't know."

"No," he says quietly, "we can't know, Peter. We can't know. But we can believe."

"Believe what? That God will save us?"

"Well, that would be a help, yes—but is there only blind faith to save us? Isn't there something else that we can do, even cooped up in here?"

"I don't know," I whisper, because I don't. They are so clever, the Franks, it's hard to know what they mean sometimes.

Mr. Frank sighs. "We have to try, Peter. We have to try and believe that *our* love can be greater than *their* hate."

"You want me to *love* them! But I *hate* them. I hate them. If I could I'd . . ."

He holds up his hand. "No, of course I don't want you to love them. What they're doing is . . . is . . . evil, but if you hate back, Peter, then will you be any better than them?"

"It doesn't feel right," is all I can say. And it doesn't. "I *want* the people who did this to suffer. I want them to die. I wish I was . . . I wish I was fighting them instead of stuck in here just . . ." I stop. I don't want to sound ungrateful to be here, but Mr. Frank just smiles.

"At your age, I'd rather have been fighting too. We need to fight them. They leave us no other choice."

"But you said we had to *love* them!"

"No! I said that you mustn't let their hate become *your* hate."

"I just want them to die!"

"An eye for an eye, a tooth for a tooth," he says, sighing.

"Yes!" I say.

He puts his hand on my shoulder. "And when we're all blind and toothless, what then, Peter?"

"I don't know," I mutter.

I hate Mr. Frank sometimes.

"And hating them is so much easier than not knowing why they hate us, isn't it?" he asks, gently.

I nod, because it's true. It is.

I wonder aloud what terrible thing it is that they avoid by hating us all so much. Mr. Frank mutters, "Yes, sometimes I wonder just what terrible thing it must be!" And then he turns and walks out of the room, still muttering, until he gets to the steps, where he turns and smiles at me. "Don't forget to do that English homework, Peter!"

That's Mr. Frank!

Otto Frank. Even in Auschwitz he was himself. "They can't kill our dreams, Peter," he said.

But he's wrong, because we all have the same dreams here. We all grind our teeth as we dream of food. Food that our teeth could bite on. Food that our bodies could grow on.

I always have the same dream: of garden peas, still green and fresh and a little hard. They're poached in Mutti's chicken stock with just a little lettuce. In my dream it's spring and she brings a great steaming tureen of them to the table—more than I could possibly ever eat. I raise the spoon to my lips. I breathe in the smell, relish the color, my mouth waters at the taste to come. I put the spoon to my lips, open my mouth and close it . . . on nothing.

My bunkmate digs his knees in my back . . . a second later his own teeth begin to grind . . . the dream spreads through the hut . . . joins the endless noise of our dreams shouting out, desperate to try and make sense of something, anything . . . no, even our dreams are not our own.

Not here.

OCTOBER 13, 1942 — PETER DREAMS OF LIESE

I'm dreaming of Liese. She's naked. She's so beautiful I can't speak, only ache. There are lines and lines of people. All of them are naked. They hold their hands between their legs. They keep their heads down. They are embarrassed.

But Liese isn't.

She's slender and beautiful. She doesn't look down at the ground like all the others. She looks up into the air above her, at the sky. Her hands don't cover herself, they hang loose by her sides. I watch, mesmerized, as slowly she lifts them. Her arms rise above her in a perfect arc. Her breasts lift. They are so beautiful. In my dream I hear music as she begins to dance. The silent people raise their bowed heads to watch as she steps out of the line.

"Stop!" shouts a guard. But she doesn't stop. She stays in perfect time to the music that only we can hear. Her face is rapt in concentration; her back is straight and tall as she balances. She takes a step forward and lifts one beautiful, naked leg high into the air, and turns. She steps lightly, slowly. Twisting and turning to the invisible music.

She stops. In front of the guard.

She lowers her arms. She's sweating. Her breath comes in gasps. She smiles up at him. I realize he's her age. My age. He stares at her breasts.

All is silence and staring.

She curtsies. Her knees bent, her arms back, her breasts a present, and then in one swift motion she sweeps her arms forward to hug him. She pulls the gun from his holster and fires. And then she turns the gun to her own head, but before she can fire, her body is already dancing under the impact of fired bullets.

"Liese! NO!"

My own scream wakes me.

I lie in the dark.

Waiting.

Breathing.

Listening for the Westertoren bells to strike the hours till morning.

Thinking about hate.

OCTOBER 14, 1942 — PETER CAN'T SHAKE OFF HIS DREAM

I wake up with an ache in my guts, a fear that she's already dead.

I make myself get out of bed.

My heart feels so heavy I don't know how to carry it. Simple things seem strange. All day I do my chores and watch myself, amazed at how I go on, just as if nothing at all was happening.

"Well done, Peter!"

"Thank you."

"Why can't you eat, Peter? Eat more! Don't you like it?"

"It's lovely. I've had enough."

At night I lie awake, scared of all the dreams that might be waiting for me in the walls. Sometimes, deep in the night, I crawl up the attic steps and stand in the darkness, waiting for the bombs to land, thinking that if I stay up here, watching, I can somehow stop them from landing on us.

Sometimes Mouschi comes and lies on my chest, purring. We watch the stars through the window.

Last night Anne left an apple on my bed. I take it up to the attic and eat it. It sounds loud in the darkness. It's crisp and cold and sweet. It's an apple. I didn't know an apple could feel like a miracle. But it does.

I eat it slowly, watching the stars move across the small piece of sky. I crawl downstairs in the first light and fall asleep.

I miss breakfast. Anne wakes me.

"Sleepyhead! You didn't even say thank you for the apple!"

I try to open my eyes. She's sitting on the bed, bouncing.

"Get off!"

But she goes on. "Get up! Get up! Get up! We have to be weighed."

I groan. Turn over. Try to block her out. My head hurts. My ears hurt. My whole body hurts with the dream; aches with it.

But she doesn't stop.

"Peter Piper picked a peck of Opekta pepper. See how good my English is getting?"

And then she tries to tickle me through the covers. I get up quickly. I can't bear being touched. She laughs and then she stops. "Peter!" she whispers. "You're still dressed."

And it's true. I can't be bothered to change. She doesn't mention it to anyone, which is decent. We are weighed. We are weighed every week. I've lost eight pounds in a week. I'm shocked. How can that happen when I'm not even doing anything?

"See?" says Mutti. "No wonder the poor boy can do nothing but sleep. He needs more food."

"We do very well here, Auguste," says Mrs. Frank.

"Of course we do, I wasn't . . ." mutters Mutti. She's still muttering as she goes past me. "Those scales can't be right, there's no way I weigh that much. It's almost as much as Edith!"

I smile.

"I've put on nineteen pounds in three months!" says Anne, proudly. What a liar! But when I look at her it's true! She has put on something. Her shape is changing.

OCTOBER 29, 1942 — THE VAN PELSES' HOME IS CLEARED

Father comes into my room.

"All right! All right!" I say quickly. "I'm getting up, I'm on my way!"

And then I look at him. He's not angry. He blinks. He holds out his hand to balance himself as he sits on the edge of the bed. He looks old. And tired. And frightening.

"What?" I whisper. "What is it?"

"Our apartment," he says. "They've taken everything."

"What?"

"The whole apartment has been emptied, Peter. There's nothing left. All our things . . ."

"Oh!" I say. "Oh, Papi!"

"Gone," he says, and he shakes his head. "Everything. A whole lifetime."

We sit there. I can't say anything. I see our apartment, our home; the rooms dance in front of my eyes.

"Ah well!" he says after a while. "At least we're still here, eh?"

I put my hand on his arm. "Sorry, Papi," I say—and I am sorry. Sorry that all the things we bought together, all the things we've made, over all the years, are gone—just like that. We have nothing to dream of going back to.

"Was it you who stole everything?" he asks. I shake my head. He smiles, or at least tries to. "I don't think I can bear to tell your mutti," he whispers.

All day I remember things, things I didn't even know we had, like the little ship in a bottle. I see exactly where it was—on the shelf in the hallway, and with the memory comes a jolt inside me at knowing it's gone.

And I don't know where.

Our apartment is empty now—with nothing left to remind anyone that we were ever there.

Father tells me not to tell Mother. That's ridiculous. How is it right for even Anne to know but not Mother? Anne does know.

"Sorry!" she says. "But honestly, what do *things* matter? You have your family, and we can trust in God."

I stare at her. I don't say anything. I can't, I'm too angry. For once she shuts up and goes away. I tell Mutti. I don't know if it's right or wrong. I don't care anymore. I just know I have to do it.

She's standing by the sink washing up after supper.

"Mutti?" I whisper in her ear, and she turns and smiles at me.

"Peter!" she says, and it's hard, hard to say the words when she's smiling and looking at me like that—so happy to have me near her. But I do it. I say the words quickly.

"Mutti, they've emptied the apartment."

At first she just closes her eyes. Closes her eyes and stands there. She turns away from me and puts her palms down on the old granite surface and takes a deep breath. I watch, helpless, as she grits her teeth, lifts her hands, and wraps her fingers around the brass tap, squeezing.

"I won't cry, I won't cry," she whispers.

Papi comes up behind her and wraps his arms around her.

"Kerli," she whispers, "our home, our . . ."

"Gusti," he says.

And he holds her.

"Please," she whispers to him, "please don't tell me we're lucky . . . don't . . . I just can't . . ."

Papi rests his head against her shoulder.

"No . . ." he says. "I won't."

"Everything?" she asks, and he nods his head against her body. She sags.

"Papi," I whisper, "do you want to lie down in my room?"

He nods, and they walk the few steps to my room.

I close the door. They're lying there together, holding each other. This is all we have now. These four rooms that aren't even ours, but borrowed from the Franks. These rooms— and each other.

NOVEMBER 8, 1942 — PETER IS SIXTEEN

Today is the eighth of November. I'm sixteen.

I hear Anne's footsteps running up the stairs. "Wake up! Wake up, Peter, aren't you excited?"

I smile.

Mutti and Papi have tried so hard. There is a board game, a razor, even though I haven't got much to shave, a cigarette lighter, and two cigarettes. I think of the piles of presents I used to have on my birthday and going out to tea in any place I chose. Now there are only these few things, and they are a miracle of effort.

I smile at Mutti. "Thank you!"

Last night she came into my room. She didn't say anything. She sat on the bed and held my hand. After a while she left. Sometimes there's nothing that can be said.

Now it's my birthday, and Anne's standing in our kitchen as though it's the most exciting day of the year, and so something has to be said, however we feel.

"Hey, cigarettes!" I lift one to my mouth and pretend to smoke it. I strut with my hand behind my back and say in German, "Ach, so, you are in hiding, yah? You say you are German? German? Can a Jew be German?"

"No!" says Anne passionately. "We'll never be German again. We're Dutch now!"

"No!" I say in German. "You are not Dutch or German. You are only Jewish!" Everybody laughs except me. I don't know why I said it. It's not even funny. It's sad.

I stand by the window and wish I could look out.

"Ah," I say. "Nothing like a good smoke first thing in the morning!" And then I turn back. "Thanks, Papi."

Mutti has the beginning of tears in her eyes. "I am . . ." she says. "I am so . . ."

"I know," I say quickly, hoping she'll stop, hoping that she won't say it. But she goes on anyway, as I know she will, as I know she has to, however much I wish she wouldn't. "I'm so *grateful* you are here," she says. I nod, and make myself smile and look at her.

"I know," I answer. And I do. I do know. I know that sometimes love is as hard to bear as hate, that it can hurt as much.

I wonder what Mr. Frank would say about that!

Anne follows me around all day.

"So, Peter van Pels, what's it like to be sixteen?" She holds an imaginary microphone to my face. "Don't worry, I can make you incognito in my diary. So you can say whatever you like, and no one will ever know it was you!" She gives me that last bit of information when I'm right at the top of the attic steps, with a sack full of beans on my back. I turn and the whole sack splits, beans pour out, bouncing everywhere. The noise is terrifying! Anne drops her imaginary microphone and covers her head as they shower down around her. At last, I've finally found a way of shutting her up! When the noise stops she lifts her head and looks up, shocked. She reminds me of a newly born chick poking its head out of its shell. We wait, the way we always do after a loud noise.

"Goodness!" says Mutti, popping her head around the door. "Lucky that wasn't heard by a passing policeman! Pick them all up, both of you, birthday or no birthday."

We start to pick up the beans.

"You looked just like a chick!" I say.

"Well you looked like a convict!"

"What? I did not!"

"You did!" She starts to laugh. "You looked just like someone who's been caught doing something bad!"

We laugh together. Quietly. We laugh so hard that we have to sit down.

So! She writes about me in her diary, does she? I wonder what she says.

Later we all go and listen to the radio.

"Peter," Father whispers. "The best birthday present! The Allies have landed in North Africa! Listen!"

I listen to Mr. Churchill's voice.

"This is not the end. It is not even the beginning of the end, but it is, perhaps, the end of the beginning!" I look over at Anne and smile. Her lips are moving, trying out the words. Over the next few days she says them over and over again. She takes the words apart and puts them back together again, and when she's finished she announces that they are perfect.

"This is not the end. It is not even the beginning of the end, but it is, perhaps, the end of the beginning. Do you get it, Peter?" she says for the millionth time.

"So it's not nearly over then?" I ask.

And for some reason everybody laughs.

Trains. A platform.

That was the beginning of our end.

The selected.

It is hard to believe there was ever a before.

Or that there could ever be an after.

Is there anybody left?

Is anyone listening?

The bodies around me still make noises, they sigh, even though they are dead.

I wait for the command.

But still it doesn't come.

WYSTAWACH!

Wake up!

The word that will make me move—get up—and go on dying.

Last week Mr. Frank announced that there would be another person in the Annex. He didn't ask me if I minded, although everybody's been talking about it.

"It's a good thing!" says Anne quickly. "And I don't mind sharing my room. I mean, what does that matter if we can save one more person?"

I stare at her. I hate the thought of another person here, even if it is Dr. Pfeffer, the dentist. He's nice enough, and the woman he lives with, Lotte, is lovely. But, still, another person—one more in the kitchen, the bathroom, the living room, in fact, everywhere.

Mutti and Papi are nodding. "It'll be difficult, but a good thing to do—Anne's right," says Papi.

Well, that's not what he said last night when the Franks had gone to bed.

I look at Margot.

"Margot will share with us, so it will inconvenience you as little as possible," says Mrs. Frank—and suddenly I feel ashamed. That means they'll have no privacy at all, and we will—especially me. It also means I can't say anything against it. We don't have the right. This isn't our Annex. I stare at my knees hoping no one can tell what I'm thinking.

I always thought I liked Dr. Pfeffer, but now I know I don't. His face looks different in the Annex. It's pudgy, and there's a dimple in his chin that moves when he speaks. He's tall and he always knows best. He's always talking about his Lotte, who he's left behind. Lucky she's not Jewish; otherwise we might have had to fit her in as well! Although I always liked her more than him.

"You'll soon remember how much you like him if you get toothache!" Mr. Frank says.

I won't.

Dr. Pfeffer walks into the Annex with the outside still clinging to him. He moves differently from the rest of us. He feels too big and too loud. He doesn't fit. He squints as though it's too dark, and leans forward to see and hear us better.

He brings news I don't want and can't ignore. He tells us how terrible it is out there; that they're rounding up Jews, netting us like fish. The south of the city where we used to live is ringed off so no one can escape. They go from house to house. Searching. Questioning. Looking for anyone hiding.

"But where are they taking us all?" asks Father.

"You've heard the rumors, haven't you?" says Dr. Pfeffer. And it makes me want to punch him. Is he enjoying it? Loving being the one with all the news.

"There's a camp near Westerbork. They shave everybody's heads. They say they're only relocating us. They say they're sending us to work camps, they say many things. Who knows what the truth is?"

There's a long silence.

"How much longer must we wait?" whispers Mutti.

"It's not only us suffering," Pfeffer says, looking around at all of us. "It's the Dutch too. Every act of resistance, the Nazis kill someone. Doesn't matter who. One moment an innocent man's walking home, the next he's up against a wall—then he's dead!"

Pfeffer shakes his head. I stroke Mouschi. Our parents ask questions, over and over again, as though they really believe that if they could only understand it properly then one day it might actually make sense.

Margot stares at them and sighs quietly.

Anne is pale and shaking, she stands up and leaves. Mouschi leaps off my lap and follows her down the stairs. After a while, so do I.

She's standing by the window in the front office, peering through the tiny gap between the blackout curtain and the glass, down onto the street below. I stand behind her and look over her shoulder onto the slice of street. It's surprising how much you can see through such a narrow gap. It's dark and the gaslight shines on the water of the canal. A line of people comes into view walking along the street—a line of Jews. They straggle, but there are plenty of guards to watch over them. The people are shadowy in the dusk. They look strangely bulky.

"They must be wearing all their clothes," whispers Anne. She has tears in her eyes.

They look so close, even though they're walking right by the canal. It feels like we could reach out and touch them. We stand very still, scared to move; scared someone might turn and notice a movement behind the dark windows.

A baby cries out and a woman in the line stops. She has a suitcase in one hand and the baby in the other. She can't carry both of them. The guard shouts at her, pushes her. She drops the suitcase and holds onto the child.

And then they're gone and the street is quiet. Only the suitcase is left, lying on its side. Anne's breath mists the glass.

Neither of us speaks.

Out of the shadows comes a skinny, ragged boy. He opens the case and begins to pull out clothes and candlesticks from it. Soon there's a silent crowd of children all pulling and fighting in the street. They come from nowhere. In seconds it's over and the street is empty again. The suitcase lies wide open. A man steps off the houseboat onto the street. Anne steps back rapidly, straight into my chest. The man feels very close. For just a moment I'm holding her in my arms where I can feel her shaking. "Sorry!" she whispers, and when we look back, the suitcase has gone.

There's only the lamplight shining on an empty street.

"Slum children!" hisses Anne, but her cheeks have tears on them, two of them glistening like small candle flames. I don't answer and she runs upstairs. I can still feel the sudden shape of her in my arms.

Mouschi twines himself around my legs.

I look out at the sliver of empty street.

All sign of the people has gone.

There's only a memory left.

My memory.

I'm frightened.

Frightened that I'll forget.

———

That night I dream. I dream I'm holding something in my hands. I can't look at it. It's bristly like a pig's back—but also somehow smooth and round. I cradle it to my chest. I hold it close like a baby. I know I must keep it safe. Treasure it. Never drop it. Hold onto it forever. It is very heavy.

I look down.

Liese's eyes stare back at me.

I'm holding her shaven head close in my hands.

These are my memories. I cannot stop them coming.

If I lay them before you, will you believe them?

You, who remain on the outside?

Are you listening?

In the Annex I could wake up from my dreams—but in the camps the dream never ends. I wake up and the nightmare is real.

I can't really believe it is happening myself, so why should you?

Do you?

Will you notice that I'm missing—or that the street looks strangely empty?

Ach! She made the right decision that woman. She didn't need her suitcase where she was going. But then again, she didn't need her child either.

NOVEMBER 18, 1942 — PETER THINKS
ABOUT GOD

It's dark when we wake up and even darker when we go to bed. We go to bed early. We get up late. Sometimes there's frost on the inside of the glass. We shiver. We wear all our clothes. Anne and Margot even wear their dressing gowns on top of everything. We do anything we can to make the time pass. We're waiting.

Waiting for news.

Waiting for the war to end.

Will we make it?

Will we run down Prinsengracht again one day? It's best not to think about it. I set myself tasks. I've drawn all the streets around here. I've drawn the route from here back to Merwedeplein, near where we used to live, with landmarks along the streets. And the tram route from Merwedeplein to Zaandvoort. I've drawn the streets around Prinsengracht.

When I'm sitting in the attic at night I picture being in a plane. I look down and see all the streets spread out around me. I imagine the chemists and the cafés. Sometimes Anne and Margot and I try to remember all the shops in a particular street—or all the stops on a tram route.

"We haven't really been to many places, have we?" Anne says.

"Well, you spent time in Aachen with Granny!" says Margot.

"Yes, but Germany and Holland, it's hardly the world, is it?"

"Where would you go, Peter?" asks Margot. I curl up on the bed and think.

"I'd like to go somewhere hot: with sand for me and maybe a forest for Mouschi!"

"It's so cold," says Anne.

"Freezing!" we all say together.

Margot sighs: "I'd go to America!"

"Why?" laughs Anne.

Margot shrugs. "I want to go somewhere new," she says. "Somewhere where none of this has happened."

Anne stares at her. "I think you're both mad. I don't ever want to leave!" she says. "I want to stay here in Holland forever!"

"And marry Mr. Ku-gler!" laughs Margot.

"Mar-got!"

"An-ne!" says Margot, exactly like Anne.

"Right!" says Anne.

I get up off the bed and out of the way. Anne and Margot go for each other. They're furious and concentrated and silent. That's what's so funny. They're lethal with the pillows, but they do it all so silently. I catch Margot's glasses before they hit the floor. Anne stops.

"Are they broken?"

"No."

"Thank goodness. Sorry."

"Quits?" asks Margot.

"Quits!" And they collapse in giggles.

"Mr. Kugler!" laughs Anne. "What an idea! How desperate would you have to be?"

For some reason they both look at me. I give Margot her glasses back and leave the room. Their giggles follow me all the way up the stairs.

"Good to see you smiling!" says Mutti, but Papi signals silently that he wants to talk. I walk into my room and a few minutes later he follows.

"Can you make a menorah, Peter?" he asks.

"The Franks'll have one," I say quickly. I don't want to think of the menorah we had at home; the thick silver candlesticks we lit each Friday evening. It's gone now, and there's nothing I can do about it.

"And what about Mutti?" he asks. "Will the Franks bring it up here each night? Will it be special to her?"

I don't answer.

"Well?" he says.

"Perhaps we could ask Miep to . . ." I look up. We both know what I was about to say—and that it's stupid.

"Right! So exactly which workshop is Miep going to walk into and ask for a Jewish menorah to be made?" Papi asks.

I breathe out. Papi sits down next to me.

"Sorry," he says. "I would make it myself, Peter, but you know how much it would mean to her if you did it."

"All right. But don't tell anyone I made it."

He stands up. "If anyone asks we'll say I made it; and thank you, Peter."

"I'll do it in the storeroom and the attic, so she doesn't know."

He smiles.

Mutti's head appears around the door: "What are you two cooking up?"

"Nothing as tasty as you are!" says Papi.

"Shh! the Franks will hear!"

"And what's wrong with that?" he replies. "Isn't a man allowed to find his wife tasty?"

"Oh, please!" I say.

"Well I wouldn't make much of a meal these days," Mutti mumbles. "We're all turning to skin and bone."

———

Later, I find a piece of paper and begin to draw. A Hanukkah menorah must have nine candleholders. I make a diagram and begin to plan.

Mr. Voskuijl, Bep's father, finds the wood for me. I would like to make it all out of one piece of wood, but that's not possible, so I do it in pieces and make joins.

I like to carve at night, downstairs in the storeroom or warehouse. I like the smell. I like being alone. I like the way that Boche, the warehouse cat, sometimes comes and sits beside me. It's good to feel my hands working again. I can see the shape in the wood; the shape that will come if I make the right cuts in the right places. I think of the wood, of its grain. I imagine where it wants to give itself to me and where it will resist. The curves grow under my hands. Eight side candles, with a raised ninth one in the center. Nine flames—one for each person in the Annex, and one for the temple.

As I carve each one I make a sign, a notch in the wood, a symbol for each person. Anne is an eye because she sees everything. Father is a smile and Mother a hand. They all come easily. Mr. Frank is a book, also easy. Margot is the hardest. She slips in and out of my mind and I have to wait and see what comes. Mrs. Frank is a needle. She's sharp, but she also mends all our things! Pfeffer's easy—a sour lemon! Margot's a wave. I don't know why. And me? In the end I make a symbol of the kippah. A Jew. If that's what I am in the eyes of the world, well then, that's what I'll be.

The best one I can be.

I will carve the menorah and burn the candles and say the Kaddish for those who are dead. And I'll make prayers of hope for us that remain. I'm praying for a miracle, just like in the temple. I carve the symbols under each candle. I dedicate one to each person. As I work I remember the prayers; I hear them in my head and whisper the words as I work—the Hanukkah prayers. I never understood why I should learn them by heart, but now I know—it's so they're always with me. My hands move to the rhythm of the words, carving them into the wood with my thoughts. At last I feel like I'm doing something.

You in your abundant mercy rose up for them in the time of their trouble, pled their cause,

Executed judgment, avenged their wrong, and delivered the strong

Into the hands of the weak,

The many into the hands of the few,

The impure into the hands of the pure,

The wicked into the hands of the righteous, and insolent ones into the hands of those living in the Torah . . . And unto your people did you achieve a great deliverance and redemption.

I whisper them again. *And unto your people did you achieve a great deliverance and redemption.*

Please, God. Deliver us.

Me and Liese, and all Jews everywhere. All the weak and the lame and everyone they hate so much. Please save us.

The menorah takes me a while to make. By the end of it I'm good friends with Boche. He watches me carefully, and when I stop working he comes closer. He reaches out a paw and touches the wood. Gently.

"Do you want it?" I ask him. "How much for it?" Boche stares at me, lifts his head, and stalks away.

"Ah!" I say. "So you think you're too grand to discuss money." But he just carries on walking. I get back to work. Soon Boche is back. Watching.

Sometimes, when my muscles are tight, I stretch out on the floor and lie very still. Boche walks on me. He starts at my feet and balances, one paw after the other all the way up from my feet to my chin. He touches his whiskers to my face, or lifts a paw and taps my eyes.

I like it best when he curls up and lies on my chest. I like the feel of his warmth and the sound of our hearts beating together in the silent dark room.

Peaceful together.

DECEMBER 3, 1942 — THE FIRST NIGHT OF HANUKKAH

The menorah is finished. Tonight is the start of Hanukkah. Mutti is making latkes. I think of our house, empty now, with no one to light the candles. I think of the fact that there was a time when I didn't know I was a Jew. Well, of course I did, but it was just one of the things I was, among many things.

Not the only thing.

I wonder how many of us are left? How many of us are lighting the candles behind dark curtains and dreaming of freedom?

I smuggle the menorah up to my room. After supper when the Franks have gone down, we stand in my doorway with it behind our backs and wait for Mutti to notice.

"What are you two doing?" she asks. We smile.

"Is there anything to smile about?" she snaps. She's sad. Perhaps we haven't got it right. Perhaps the sadness is too much? I take a step back, but Papi just says, "Yes, there is, come here," and makes her stand in front of us. I'm worried though, what if it's not right? I mean, it's not beautiful or silver. I know it can never replace the one that Oma, her mother, gave her. I mean, how could it?

"Peter," says Papi.

Slowly I bring it out from behind my back. Mutti gives a gasp. She stares at it and slowly reaches out her hands to take it. She runs her hands all over it and looks up at me.

"I . . . I . . ." she stutters, the tears filling her eyes.

"I know it's not beautiful, like Oma's and I . . ."

"Peter, I . . . you made it?" she asks.

I nod.

"I . . . I don't know what . . ."

"Say it, woman!" laughs Papi, and then she starts to cry properly. The tears running down her face and the words coming out like hiccups in between them.

"I never thought I could ever . . . I was so . . . I didn't think I could ever feel the same about another menorah, and I was so . . . and you two . . . and oh, oh, Peter . . . Thank you . . . it's beautiful!"

It's not really, but I'm glad she thinks so.

DECEMBER 12, 1942 — PETER AND HIS PARENTS CELEBRATE THE FESTIVAL OF HANUKKAH

We keep the menorah in the kitchen. Each night, when the Franks have gone down, we light a candle. We don't mention it to them. I say a prayer, silently, each night, for the person whose candle is lit. What else can I do? We pray quickly because candles are precious. I like it being just the three of us. I like the look of Mutti and Papi's faces, serious in the candlelight. I like the way we say the words together—and then we have a few seconds of silence, and pray alone. The night I pray for Mr. Frank, the candle won't blow out. Mutti has to try twice!

When it's my turn to pray for me, it's hard. All I can say is keep me alive. Oh Lord, please keep me alive—and Liese. Help us meet again one day. But I keep hearing the same question: Why? And there's no answer, because why should I survive, when so many are dying? There's no reason.

That's the truth.

By the time it's the last night of Hanukkah the candles are nearly stumps! The Franks light them and we all say the prayer together before we eat. They say it quickly and then it's over. For them, that's Hanukkah. Anne was more excited about celebrating St. Nicholas for the first time. When they leave, Mutti relights a candle and stares into its flame. I know that she's praying for me, thanking God that I'm alive. And do you know what? She chose the right candle. She leans forward to blow it out—and stops. Her tears glisten in the flickering light.

"I . . . I . . ." she whispers, "I can't!" So I lean forward and blow it out myself. She smiles.

"Do you think if we left it, it would burn for eight days?" she asks. She laughs as though she's being silly. But she isn't. I don't know where the words come from. I'm so bad at words.

"We need a miracle," I say. And she nods.

"Good night, Peter."

"Good night." And Papi hugs us both. I go to my room and Hanukkah is over.

———

When I wake up the next morning my hands feel empty. I've got nothing to do. I go down to the storeroom and search for Boche. I can't find him anywhere. Sometimes he spends whole days out on the streets, scavenging. When he comes home, he smells of air. He smells of streets. I sink my face into his fur and breathe it in. It's lovely. It's full of the damp wood-smoke autumn smell of Amsterdam. Of canals and streetlights.

Of outside.

MARCH 18, 1943 — TURKEY'S JOINED
THE WAR!

"Now they'll invade. At last, some action!" says Mutti.

"And maybe some cigarettes!" says Papi.

"Honestly!" says Mrs. Frank. "They're not fighting the war for us alone, you know!"

A silence.

"No, they're not," says Mr. Frank. "But perhaps it's hard to remember that, when we're locked up in here, waiting."

"Why do they call it cleansing?" Anne asks suddenly. She doesn't notice the silence, the sadness that lands on us all whenever she mentions things so suddenly, without warning. Mr. Frank sighs.

"Why do you think, Anne?" he asks, but she doesn't answer, just asks abruptly, "Would they really cleanse children?"

"We don't know exactly what's happening, Anne, only that it's bad."

He doesn't want to say it, I'm thinking. He doesn't want to say that yes, of course they would cleanse children. And precious, clever, know-it-all Anne can't see it.

"But we do know!" She says it too loudly. Even though it's

suppertime and all the workers have gone home, she should still be quiet. "We know that they want to get rid of us, and so what are they doing with us when they round us up?"

Everyone's silent. Even Anne notices it, but maybe she thinks it's that we disagree with her. Maybe she can't see that questions are something we ask ourselves alone, and at night. We ask them when all we can hear is the wind at the window and the church bells striking the hours. We don't ask them out loud. Only Anne does that—and then she feels bad about it, and so suddenly it's everyone else's fault.

She leaps up and flounces down the stairs.

"Anne!" says her father.

"Be careful on those stairs!" hisses Mrs. Frank. Anne stops and turns to her.

"You don't care about me hurting myself," she hisses. "You're just worried about us being found!"

"Anne!" Mr. Frank loud-whispers.

"You've raised a very spoiled child," mutters Mutti.

Margot stares at her plate very hard; she breathes in through her nose and out through her mouth. I stand up and ask to be excused.

"Now, there's a polite boy," smiles Mutti.

"Good Lord, come down and give me a cigarette for my trials!" mutters Papi. I think Margot grins beneath her hair.

I'm blushing again. I hate it when Mutti praises me in front of the others —especially for something so stupid.

———

Bad news, Turkey hasn't joined the war; instead it's just having a think about not being neutral. It might not have to think so hard if it was Jewish.

MARCH 24, 1943 — PETER DISCOVERS A BREAK-IN

Sometimes I can't stand the atmosphere in the Annex. Margot feels the same, I know. She deals with it by doing chores and reading. If it's the evening or the weekend I go and find Boche down in the storeroom, or even all the way down to the warehouse on the ground floor.

I can only go downstairs on weekends, or evenings, of course. At other times the office and warehouse workers are around. I like slipping silently in my socks all the way down the secret staircase. I like getting further and further away from the Annex. I have to come down at night, though, to bolt the door, and back again in the morning to unbolt it so Mr. Kugler can use his key.

It's dark in the storeroom, just like it is everywhere in the Annex—only darker, in fact, because the windows are completely blacked out. And it smells. "It smells of the world, Peter!" Mr. Frank says—and he's right. I can identify the smells now. Pepper especially. It makes the cats sneeze.

Anne and Margot hate it down here, they think it's creepy. That's good because it means I get it all to myself. It takes a while for your eyes to adjust in the dark, but then it's fine. And it's quiet. Just me and Boche, purring, I like it.

I'm playing with Boche, kneeling down in the nearly dark and holding a bean in one of the hands behind my back.

"Guess?" I whisper, and show Boche both hands. He leans forward, sniffs at my hands. His whiskers tickle. He sits back and stares and then delicately lifts a paw and taps my left hand. I turn it over. Open it. The bean is there. "Clever Boche!" I whisper and we nod at each other and begin again. I hide the bean behind my back, bring my hands around, but suddenly Boche doesn't want to play—he turns his face away.

"Hey!" I whisper. "Mouse?" But he doesn't answer, just stalks toward the warehouse door and then back again—pushing his head hard against my knees.

"What?" I rub his head. His skull feels so small beneath his fur. I don't like that. He pushes and pushes against my hands. I kneel down and look into his eyes: "What is it?" But he twists his head away from me and stalks toward the door again . . . the sound crashes through the air.

I jump. I leap up and stand in the dark, staring, with my heart beating hard. What was that? I'm not used to loud sounds. For a split second I can't make any sense of what's happening. Then my brain begins turning, fast. A barrel's fallen over in the warehouse. Someone must be in there. Boche was trying to tell me someone was there. Did they hear me? Do they know I'm here? Was I quiet enough? Boche stares at me. I stare back.

I keep very, very still. I watch as the handle of the door turns. It turns all the way around, and then the door's rattled, hard.

I step back.

Who is it? If they were Nazi sympathizers or the green police they would just come in, wouldn't they? They must be thieves. We can negotiate with thieves. Or can we? People are starving. What price eight Jews? I don't know. I don't know much at all.

I watch as Boche strolls to the door, scratches at it, and lets out a loud meow.

I turn and run.

I slip silently and fast up the stairs. It feels like it takes forever.

The Franks are in their sitting room/bedroom. I whisper to Mr. Frank. Anne realizes what's happening straightaway, she starts to shake. She turns white and Margot wraps an arm around her quickly. Mr. Frank rises swiftly and we go downstairs. He stops in the front office and warns Mutti to turn off the radio and go upstairs. She glances at me, is about to reach out and hug me until she sees the warning in my eyes—her hand drops back to her side.

"Ready?" whispers Mr. Frank. I nod, proud that he hasn't sent me away, hasn't looked for Father. We creep down the stairs and wait at the bottom, listening. I realize we have no weapons, nothing except our fists. I raise them. The dark is complete. We stand and listen to each other breathing. There's no other sound, nothing.

And then a door bangs.

Bang! And another—bang! Like a gunshot. And Mr. Frank whispers, "I'm going to warn them upstairs!" He disappears. I'm alone.

I step forward, fists raised, but nothing happens, so I follow Mr. Frank. Dr. Pfeffer is in his room. The one he shares with Anne. "Get upstairs!" I say. It comes out terse and rude.

"How dare you talk to me like that, you young . . ." I walk up to him, my heart beating fast with fear. I hold him by his shirt under his throat. I hold him too tight. Maybe it's because I'm scared. Maybe not.

"There are people in the warehouse! Get upstairs, now!" I hiss at him. He signals with his hands. I realize he can't move until I let him go. He runs up the stairs, Noisily. Idiot.

I follow him.

Silently.

Everyone except Father is in the Franks' sitting room. One by one we creep up to the kitchen—and we wait.

Listening. Father coughs. Margot gets him some medicine. She's swift and quiet and brave. We wait. Anne is still shaking. White and quiet for once.

"Are you all right?" I whisper.

"When I heard you coming back up the stairs," she says, "I . . . I . . . didn't know that . . . I mean I wasn't sure it was you and Father . . . I thought it might be . . ."

"Shhh!" whispers Margot. "Not now, Anne." We all know what she thought. That it was them, coming for us. Papi coughs again. Then apologizes. Then coughs. Then goes red with the effort of trying not to cough. Then apologizes. And then coughs again—until I want to strangle him.

"Did you turn off the radio?" I whisper to Mutti. She nods, but Anne hears me.

"The radio's still there!" she cries. "What if the air-raid warden comes around and searches the building?" she whispers in horror. "He'll see eight chairs around an illegal radio tuned in to Britain . . . and they'll . . ."

"Anne! Shhh. We can't do anything about it right now," Margot whispers. I look up at her. She's so quiet normally, but now things are desperate she's brave and calm, and it's Anne who's falling apart.

Mr. Frank stands up. "I'm going to see if anything's happening down there." I stand up with him. Father too.

We wait to see if Pfeffer will come with us, but he stays sitting with the women. I reach for a hammer. Father puts his coat on and picks out a chisel. Mr. Frank takes nothing. We go down into the dark and wait. Nothing. Not a sound.

"They must have gone," whispers Father.

We creep back to the front office and replace the chairs, hide the radio, and hope a warden doesn't notice the break-in and come searching. We go back upstairs and wait.

It's all we ever do.

Wait.

I hide the hammer under my bed, just in case.

As soon as I fall asleep the dreams begin. Men in shiny helmets, like insects, crawl from the walls. All through the night I wake, listen, wait. Dream.

At breakfast we're all so tired we can barely speak—except for Anne, of course.

"Did you listen for the bells last night?" she asks. "I listened all night but they didn't come. I wonder where they are?"

"Ah, so that's why I was so disturbed!" says Mutti, slapping her thigh.

"Ach!" says Father. "Like children, those church bells—at first they plague you, and then you get so used to them that you can't live without them!"

Everyone smiles.

"Mmm, and there I was thinking I couldn't sleep because

we'd had a break-in," says Mr. Frank drily, hiding behind yesterday's newspaper.

"Bells, what bells?" asks Mutti. "I've never heard any bells."

Mrs. Frank laughs. "Honestly, Auguste, we all know you are only teasing!"

"It's called a carillon," says Margot suddenly. "You know, when there's a peal of bells, in English, from the French, I mean. It's called a carillon of bells. Isn't that lovely?" She stops, and blushes.

"That's beautiful," I say. I whisper the word to myself. "Carillon."

"Well," says Anne, "they've stopped ringing. I wonder why." Then she makes up a story, right then, about how the bells have had enough and are refusing to ring for the Nazis.

"They'll only ring on the day all Jews are liberated," she says, and takes another mouthful of what we call food these days.

"What are you looking at?" she asks me.

"How do you do that?" I ask back.

"Do what?"

"Make things up like that?"

She shrugs. "How do you go downstairs when you think a burglar might be down there? I couldn't!"

"Mmm," smiles Mr. Frank. "Thank goodness we're all different."

"Except if we weren't, there wouldn't be a war," says Mutti.

We're all silent for a minute thinking about that—and then for some reason we all start laughing.

I like it when that happens.

MARCH 27, 1943 — PETER AND MARGOT
CHAT IN THE ATTIC

Why do I have to learn English? Will the British or Americans kill me if I thank them in Dutch? And French, what for—I mean, I like the sound of it. I like saying the words, but I don't really care what they mean. I already speak Dutch and German, isn't that enough?

Répondez, s'il vous plaît. That's how you say RSVP in long-hand—it means send a reply, please. Margot and Anne have learned shorthand. They pass each other notes written in it, read them, and giggle. It is *so annoying*.

"At least they're learning something!" says Mrs. Frank, giving me a look as sharp as her needles.

"To be rude, it seems!" snaps Mutti. "I wonder where they get that from?"

I stand up.

"What do you think, Peter?" asks Anne. "Does it bother you, us writing notes? *RSVP, tout de suite.*"

"Please, may I be excused?" I say, and leave.

"*Il répond, ça c'est vrai,*" laughs Anne.

"*Oui, avec son pieds.*" Margot smiles.

I don't answer. I don't know what they're talking about. Perhaps my feet smell—*pieds*—that's feet, isn't it?

I stand in the attic. I make myself breathe long and slow and try not to feel angry. I look up into the tree, it's full of buds. I wish I could reach out and touch them. I wish I had a handful of them. I wish I were sitting in the branches of the tree swinging my legs in the air, with Liese.

I wish a lot of things.

But none of them will happen.

Sometimes I wish Anne would disappear in a puff of smoke.

And then I feel bad for wishing that, because we *are* disappearing. All the time. We've just heard that all Jews must be cleansed from German-occupied territories. We are to be "cleansed in north and south Holland" between the first of May and the first of June.

"We are to be routed out by Herr Rauter!" says Mr. Frank in English. Anne laughs as though she understands the joke. Perhaps she does, perhaps she's so clever that she'll be able to save herself.

But how will they cleanse us? That's what Anne asked and what I want to know. Cleansing makes me think of ant-hills and poison. It makes me feel like I want to put on boots and crush each Nazi like a beetle beneath my feet. Is this what Mr. Frank means when he says I shouldn't be filled with their hate? Does it make me as bad as they are?

I reach behind the rafters and pull out one of Papi's cigarettes. I light it. The smoke makes me cough.

"All right?" asks Margot. She appears so silently I jump. I didn't hear her.

"Cleansed," I whisper. It's like that with Margot. She's so quiet you can just go on thinking. "They're cleansing us, like cockroaches."

"We *are* cockroaches—to them," she says. But she even says that quietly, like it's a fact, not anything to get especially upset about. She sits next to me and leans forward, breathes in the smoke.

"Want some?" I ask. "Just make sure you don't breathe it in—it makes you cough!"

But she shakes her head. "I just wanted to know what it's like. I hate it. It smells."

We're silent for a while.

"At least the Dutch are still on our side," she whispers. I nod. A few days ago the Dutch resistance dressed up as German officers and blew up the labor exchange! Even better, when the firemen came they kept the hoses going and deliberately drenched everything as well as putting the fire out. So all the records are ruined. We both look at each other and smile.

"We're not cockroaches, are we, Margot?" I don't know why I ask her, the words just come out.

"No, Peter," she says, "but they try to make us feel like we are, and if they succeed, then they've won." I stare at her. I don't think I've ever heard her say so many words, or sound so passionate. She blushes. "At least that's what Father says," she adds quickly, and then she turns away.

"Peter, where do you think they send us?" she asks suddenly. She doesn't look at me, and she doesn't wait for an answer either before she asks the next question. "And what do you think they do with us?"

I don't answer. I glance at her, a quick glance. Her glasses glint in the light. I look away. It's like walking on hot coals, asking questions. I look up at the buds on the tree. I don't look at Margot.

"I don't know," I whisper, "but I suppose . . . I think, cleanse means, clean out, get rid of . . . it means kill. I suppose."

"But why?" she whispers.

I shake my head. "Your father says they're so full of hate for themselves they have to get rid of it somehow."

"Peter!" she whisper-yells and I realize my fingers are burning. I drop the cigarette. I'd forgotten it was still in my hand.

"Quick!" she says. We crush it, over and over until every single spark has gone.

"Imagine!" is all Margot says. And we do. We both know

if the building caught fire we'd be flushed out like animals—
or burned to death. We both know how trapped we are. How
helpless.

Margot tries to smile and then turns to go. I haven't answered her question. The question we all ask ourselves, over
and over, but never speak out loud, except Anne.

"Margot?" She looks up.

"I . . . I don't know why us," I say.

She shakes her head. "Neither do I, but sometimes . . ."
She stops.

"What, Margot?"

She sits on the top of the stairs and puts her chin in her
hands. I wait.

"Sometimes I'm actually glad it's not just us," she says. "I
mean that it's others too. That they hate anyone who isn't exactly like them, it . . . oh, I don't know!"

"Neither do I."

"Do you think that makes me bad?" she asks. "I mean,
being glad that other people suffer?"

I laugh. "You, Margot? Bad? You're the sweetest person
anywhere, ever."

"Oh!" she says. "I . . . you . . . ?"

"Margot, you couldn't be bad if you tried."

"I think I could," she says slowly, thoughtfully, as though
it was something she should try.

I start to laugh. "Not if you have to think about it that hard!"

She smiles suddenly. "Perhaps you're right," she says.

"I am."

"Oh well, time to do my reading." And she goes down the steep stairs. I watch her. She goes slowly. She goes carefully, so as not to make a noise. She does it like that to keep herself safe. She does it like that not to put herself, or any of us, in danger. That's the way we live—and sometimes it makes us want to scream. Sometimes it makes me want to crush people beneath my boots.

I grind the rest of the cigarette butt to dust under my heel. I grind it till there's nothing left. I pick up the dust and blow it away. And then I turn and follow her down the stairs.

———

That night I dream I'm a foot—a great big foot, stepping on soldiers. I feel their helmets crush like beetle shells beneath my boots. The ground is slippery and red. I jump in blood—like puddles. And with each step a word rises: Hate . . . Hate . . . Hate . . . Hate, in a puff of smoke that moves and changes, and however hard I try to stamp it out, it eludes me.

I wake up suddenly in the dark. I open my eyes wide and wait for a speck of light to reach them.

Nothing.

I listen for the bells to help me measure out the hours of darkness left.

They're gone.

The world is silent.

And I'm angry.

Are we to be left with anything, anything at all? Is this all I am?

A hole in the silence.

You knew, boy. You always knew. Somehow, even then, you sensed it.

The fear.

That they might succeed and wipe us off the face of the earth.

Our history gone as easily as our homes were cleared.

But still, it's hard to believe that I lived your life once.

Were you really once me?

And I you?

DECEMBER 1943, HANUKKAH

I've been here too long. Sometimes it feels as though my life before now was a dream. Sometimes it feels as though the thought of any future can only ever be a dream, although I don't say so.

Outside, the sky is blue and cold. The branches of the chestnut tree are bare again, except for high up on the left-hand side, where some brown, curled leaves cling to a branch. I take bets with Anne. She says they will hang on all winter and still be there to be pushed off by the new leaves in spring. I say the wind will blow them away before February.

I hope she's right.

I'm trying to find the menorah. I pull it out of a box. It's a whole year since I made it. Some days were sunny, some were warm, some cold. Some happy, some sad, some angry, and some bored.

Slowly I brush away the dust on the candlesticks, and stare at the symbols I carved.

A whole year.

I am seventeen now. Seventeen. I've never made love to a girl—or only in my dreams. In my dreams I remember every inch of Liese: the curve of her waist, the imagined weight of her breasts, the apricot feel of her skin, and the light in her eyes.

In reality I know nothing.

I hold the menorah in my hand. I wonder what happened to my prayers. Where did they go?

So many of us have disappeared. We try not to think of it, to talk of it. We live. We go on. We cling like the brown leaves to the tree.

A whole year gone. I never thought I'd still be here in 1944.

I've stood in the attic and watched a dogfight, seen bombs fall and fires start. In autumn, I watched the geese leave. I heard them each morning, flying over the attic. They flew past the windows, calling, flying into the sun.

Outside.

Margot came and we watched together. Most mornings we could only hear them—but one day, one day they flew straight overhead, right above us. Twelve of them flying in formation like a long open wing— a dark line against the sky, disappearing.

"It feels like a miracle," Margot said.

"What does?" I asked.

"That they can still do that. That they can still fly away."

And it does. I know what she means. When you're trapped

like we are, it *is* a miracle that the world goes on outside. It feels strange that flowers still grow, or that Miep can walk outside and then return. Because our world has stopped spinning. It's stuck. There is being alive and there is living. We are alive. Perhaps one day we'll live again.

"Ah, living!" says Papi. "Maybe one day that will come."

We're all still here, all eight of us. Like the fact that the geese still fly—that's a miracle too.

It's hard to believe in miracles. It's easier just to get on with the day-to-day things, things that I know can be done. I've tried so hard to have faith, but I think for someone like me, it needs real outside air to keep it going.

I can't believe in a God that lets this happen. I won't believe in a God who says Jews are his chosen people.

I don't want to cause hurt and I don't want to be persuaded. I can't believe that to be Jewish is better or worse than to be any other thing, and if God does choose, then how can he be any better than us? Because that's what *they* do, isn't it? Only *they* choose to hate us best, just like God chooses to love us best.

Both are right, or both are wrong.

And we're only people—that's what I keep thinking. We're only people, just like all the people who walk past the Annex, never looking up, never knowing we're here waiting for our world to begin again.

I don't know.

I still love the candles. I'll still say the words of the prayer. I don't want anyone to know how I feel. I don't want to talk about it.

This year I will think of each of us, and what we have left.

Of Margot whom I sometimes think I could love.

Of Anne and her eyes that can still sparkle.

Of Mutti: silly and wonderful and annoying and kind.

Of Papi with his jokes and his temper and his trying to let me be a man.

I'll try to remember all the things I've forgotten I once knew, like how it feels to laugh out loud without fear.

Or how legs can ache after a long walk.

Or choosing what to eat!

Or the right to hate school rather than long for it.

Sometimes, even now, I wake up and turn over, expecting Mutti's voice to call up the stairs and tell me to get ready for school. Then I open my eyes and see the walls and remember.

That I'm here.

That's what I would pray for, if I believed it would make any difference. To get up in the morning and walk down Zuider-Amstellaan on my way to the Lyceum. In my mind it would be autumn. Leaves would be floating on the canals. The sun would shine. The world would be golden, and a friend would shout: "Hey! Van Pels!" I'd raise my hand and wave.

"See you at Oasis later!" And I'd nod and walk on.

That's it! That's my dream. My dream of an outside where I can live every day like that's all it is—just another day.

"Peter!" I turn around. Papi is standing there.

"If you don't come down with that menorah it's *you* your mutti will set alight!" He comes to stand before me. Together we look out the window. It will be dark soon. We are halfway through a winter. It is always dark in the Annex, but it's worse somehow in winter—cold and damp. Even Anne stops trying to be so bright and cheerful.

Papi smiles and runs his fingers over the washing drying there. The clothes are old and worn. Mrs. Frank is ruining her eyes with sewing in this light, but still the holes grow. We all have our jobs: Mr. Frank holds our minds together and Mrs. Frank keeps our clothes together. Mutti keeps our bodies together and Papi mends things and makes us groan out loud and smile at his jokes.

Still, I wish they didn't all argue so much.

"Do you remember Anne hanging out all her papers to dry?" he says. I nod. "Catholic Maria de Medici next to Protestant William of Orange, such *rassenschande,*" he says. "Hitler would never approve." I smile, it's one of his better jokes, as jokes go, but they all wear off after a while.

"Ach," he says, and he holds a holey vest between his fingers. "Look at this. A disgrace! Your mother used to wear such beautiful things. So beautiful, Petel. Pink silk, you should have seen . . ." and he turns quickly and stares out of window. In the silence a bird flies white across the sky. Father's back is very straight, and then he smiles. I can't see the smile but I can feel it. He begins to whisper to himself.

I don't move.

I listen.

"Ah, Gusti, you looked so beautiful. So beautiful I can't tell you." And then he speaks aloud, "Layers, Peter! That's what they wrapped brides in then. Layers, like a present for us to unwrap. And everything the best! She wore silk. Pink like her young cheeks. She keeps it, even here. Ach, so tiny, a handkerchief of silk. You know, the night she heard our house was emptied she held it in her hands all night. A thin piece of silk. Ach, what madness is this, eh? That I'm talking to my own son about his mother!"

I don't move. I don't smile. I want him to go on, and I want to say: "Don't you know, Papi? Don't you think I can hear you both at night?"

Especially the night our house was emptied.

He turns from the window; the vest is shredded in his hands. Does he think I can't see it? His sorrow—his longing for the past?

Well, at least you've had a past, I think. *I haven't, or not much of one!*

"Bring down the menorah then," he says.

And he turns and is gone.

JANUARY 5, 1944 — PETER IS IN HIS ROOM, TRYING TO ESCAPE ANNE

Sometimes the way Anne looks at me unnerves me. It reminds me of measuring things, like sizing up a piece of wood, ready to make the first cut. I'm not sure if I like it, or maybe I do. I don't know.

She's in my room. She holds her cheek in her hand and tips her head sideways. I don't know who she is being today but it's obvious she's here to stay. I sigh and get off my bed (the most comfortable place to sit), and go and sit by the desk. I try to carry on with the crossword, but she keeps bouncing up off the bed and staring over my shoulder, telling me the answers. I write them in.

"What does Margot do in here?" she asks.

"Margot doesn't come in here, she goes up to the attic."

"Oh!"

Every time I look up, she stares straight into my eyes. It's odd. I'm getting a squint from trying to stare around her. I sigh. I wish it was Liese sitting there.

Anne is talking. The words go on and on. She's lecturing me about my blushing. Telling me I'll stop one day, that she's read an article, so she knows. She tells me all about it. I nod. I can't speak. I can't really hear the words. I can only see

119

Liese's face. The way her eyes used to light up when they landed on me. I never blushed with Liese.

I look hard at the crossword, concentrate, try to find meanings. After a while Anne finally stands up. I stand up too, and say goodbye. Can she tell how desperate I am for her to leave?

I fall onto the bed. I curl up. I hold my head in my hands. But the picture of Liese won't come. Instead I keep seeing Anne: her odd hair, her strange look. I feel angry—angry that she came into my room, angry that I'm too polite to ask her to leave, angry that she's gotten in between me and my memories of Liese.

Where are you, Liese?

Are you alive or dead?

Are you already up there somewhere, looking down on me?

And then the tears do come.

Hot and scalding.

JANUARY 24, 1944 — ANNE IS
ATTRACTING EVERYONE'S ATTENTION

Anne says she has decided: New year, new Anne. Today she came up to supper with her hair tied back tight and a strange bit sticking up at the front. At least it was sticking up for a while, until it fell into her eyes.

Margot smiled at me over the rotten kale (don't think; just put it in your mouth and swallow). We don't say anything. The parents say enough.

"Who are you today, Anne? Give us a twirl!" says Mutti.

"It looks ridiculous!" says Mrs. Frank. "Would you be seen on the street like that?"

There's a silence, but Anne just laughs. "I'd be seen on the street in anything if I could just get out there!" she snaps back.

"Anne!" says Mr. Frank. Margot puts her head down and breathes out. Anne flounces away. Margot picks up Anne's plate.

"Put it down, Margot," her father says. She stares at him from behind her glasses. "Sit," he says gently. She sits down. He goes and gets Anne, who sits back at the table in silence until we've finished and then clears the table.

"There is absolutely no reason why your sister should

121

clear up after you and your affectations!" I hear him whisper to her. Anne nods and swallows. She holds her head up, but her fallen hair makes her look ridiculous.

"I'll help," I say, and together we do the washing up. Margot dries. You'd be amazed at how silently we manage it in the half-dark.

"You don't have to help, Margot," says Anne, but Margot doesn't answer.

"Doesn't everyone think you're perfect enough already?" Anne hisses. Margot sighs.

Anne giggles. "You thought Boche was a girl, didn't you, Peter?"

"Leave him alone, Anne!" says Margot. I wash another plate.

"He did! He thought he was going to have babies!" I blush some more.

"I hadn't checked," I say. "He had a swollen stomach."

"Everyone makes mistakes, Anne, even you!" Margot mutters, but Anne ignores her.

"Can you tell whether it's a boy or a girl? Do you know how?" she asks.

"Mmmm," I say.

"I am here," hisses Margot.

"Are you?" asks Anne.

"Cats!" I say, and then blush.

If they were cats their backs would be arched and they would be showing each other their teeth. Or at least Anne would. Margot would just stick her tail in the air and walk away. Which is what I do as soon as we've finished. "Come down with me if you want, and I'll show you he's a boy," I say. I don't think they'll come, not really, but Anne follows me down the stairs. When we get there Boche isn't around. I sit against the wall and we wait. I don't want to talk. This is my place, my quiet place. I don't really know what to do with Anne in it. After a while we leave.

Later I go down on my own. I'm trying to dig out a picture on some old cork tiles. It's good because it takes a long time. Down each side I've cut out a curtain and a slice of window. I'm drawing the houseboat across the canal. Well, cutting it out really. It's very basic. I'm not very good at it, but I like it because it takes time. Anything that takes time is good.

It's so dark in the room that I almost do it by feel. I hear the footsteps, even though they're very quiet. I hide the work quickly and pick up Boche. He yowls and Anne pokes her head through the door. Her hair's tied back, with just a few curls escaping, and she has her ragged old dressing gown over her clothes. It's cold. Sometimes we wear nearly everything we possess—and if we're lucky the old holes cover up the new ones.

"Hello!"

"Hello!"

She comes over to Boche and holds her hands out.

"What are you doing with him?" she asks. Boche twists away from her and I dig my fingers into his thick fur, running my hands along his spine the way he likes. After a bit he settles. When I look up, Anne's staring at me—at my hands.

"What?" I ask. I wish she'd go away. I like being alone in the dark, feeling a picture take shape. I like the sound of Boche yawning and prowling.

"So, how do you tell if he's a he?" she asks, and blushes.

"Oh, right, well it's right here."

I tip Boche over and show her.

"He's a male cat, you can tell because he doesn't have teats, and he has this instead."

I point, it's hard to say the word.

"Oh!" says Anne, "and is it the same in humans?"

"Yes," I say, looking hard at Boche, who's scrabbling to turn over, "although not furry!"

We both start to laugh.

It's obvious she doesn't know much. She asks a lot of questions, mostly about how it's possible not to get pregnant. She asks if Mutti and Papi only wanted one child. It's nice to be the one who knows a little bit more than she does for a change.

Boche begins to tap my hand with his paw; he wants to play. I hide a bean in my hand.

"Peter?" Anne blurts out. "Women and men are different, aren't they?"

"Yes," I smile. I wonder what it is Anne wants to know. When she wants to know something, nothing will stop her, not even the fact that she's obviously embarrassed. But then she says, "Well I know that *geschlechsteil* means sexual organ, and I know the woman's name for it, but what's the man's called?"

I'm so shocked I don't say anything for a while.

I'm shocked by the word.

I'm shocked that she's asking me.

I'm shocked to be talking to a girl about boys.

"You know all about Greek," I say, "but not about this?"

"Well," she says, and smiles, "you can only get so much from books."

I don't know what to say. I don't want to get into trouble. What will Mr. Frank think of me, discussing the word *penis* with his daughter? Should I be having this conversation?

"I'll ask my parents," I blurt out. "After all they're the ones with the experience in these matters!"

She nods seriously, not realizing it was a joke. Thank goodness for that. I don't want Mr. Frank to think I'm corrupting his daughter. Although it feels more like she's corrupting me.

I pick up the key and head for the stairs.

"*Can* you ask your parents?" she says.

"Mmm," I mutter.

"It's just that I heard your mother say that she never discussed such things with you."

"You heard that?"

"I hear a lot," she says.

"Well"—I take deep breath—"perhaps Mutti just didn't want to hear what a fat flirt she was who should know better than to tell her son such things!"

I give her a big smile and run up the stairs.

FEBRUARY 1, 1944 — PETER CATCHES
SIGHT OF THE DIARY

Anne's sitting at the kitchen table, scribbling. For a moment I think I might get a glance at the famous diary she always says she's writing, but all she's doing is writing her name over and over. Signing it, like she's practicing for when she's famous. She stops and sighs. A deep sigh, right up from her guts. "Do you think anyone will ever know about us?" she asks, but quietly, because there's always someone around who might hear. And if our parents do hear us ask a question, they leap on it like a cat with a rat, and pull it to pieces until there's nothing left for us to even *want* to think about. I sit down next to her.

"I don't know," I say. "What do you mean? Just us, in here, or the whole of the race?"

"Oh no!" she says, and she half smiles. "Just us, in here, in the Annex. Thinking about any of the rest of it's just too depressing." She's whispering. I'd never noticed before that whispering is intimate.

"It's not forever," I say. "Hopefully."

"No?" she asks, and she looks sad. Sad and thin and tired and young. And the dark circles under her eyes look darker.

I ruffle her hair. I don't know why, it just feels like she needs comforting. She smiles at me.

I look at the exercise book and she closes it quickly. Ah, it must be the diary! I look away.

"Sometimes," I say, "I look at something I've made and wonder if it'll still be here when I've gone."

I don't know if that's what she means, but it's the best I can do.

"That's different," she whispers.

"Different from what?"

"From words and stories and ideas." I notice our heads are nearly touching. I reach out for the diary, stroke it. She doesn't stop me.

"But this is still a thing, isn't it?" I ask. "I mean, these words, they'll still be here, won't they, even if we . . . if we aren't?" I manage to say.

She stares at me, and it feels good. It feels like I've surprised her.

"They burned books," she whispers. "They burned them, in piles. Loads of them."

I nod. "I know, Anne, but it's like your father says, they can't burn ideas. Not all of them." She nods again. And then she lifts her head and stares at me.

"Why don't you talk more, Peter?" she says. I smile. Will

128

there ever be a time when there's *not* a question inside Anne Frank?

"Well, look what happens when I do. I just get tongue-tied and blush, or it comes out angry. Anyway, most of the time I just wish I was still two years old and could punch someone instead of talking!"

"Like Dr. Pfeffer?" she asks.

I nod. He irritates me.

"I talk *too* much!" she says. And because there's nothing much else to do, and because it feels like she wants me to, I try to talk. I talk like I stroke Mouschi, to soothe him. I talk about nothing. I talk because Anne's eyes remind me of how I felt when I first got here, alone and scared and unable to think about any of it. She curls up on the sofa and gazes at me, and somehow that makes it easier, because it doesn't really matter what I say, does it? Anne will probably just turn it into something else anyway. Something that suits her better!

FEBRUARY 3, 1944 — PETER CAN'T FIND
THE WORDS

I wish I had words like Anne and Margot. I wish I could write instead of draw. I wish I could describe how it feels to be stuck in here. A teacher once told us about torture. She said it isn't just the pain that hurts; it's the knowing. Knowing that the pain will happen. It's like that in here. We all know, but we have to pretend we don't, otherwise, why bother? Why go on if you're just going to die anyway?

Will we make it?

The question gnaws at us. It eats us up from the inside out. It's like a scratching behind the walls at night. You want to jump out of bed and find it. You want to kill the mouse or rat that's doing it. But you want to stay asleep, too, warm and cozy in your bed.

Pretending it's not there.

But our parents can't stop worrying at the rat, picking it up and shaking it between their teeth. When will the invasion come? Why aren't the British faster? Will it be the British, or the Americans? Do we care? No! What if the food runs out? How strong are the Germans? How long will the Dutch resist? How much for eight Jews? It goes on day after day, the same questions, the same arguments.

Endlessly.

It really looks like it might be ending. Everyone thinks it will come soon. Everyone is excited. Everyone is scared.

I think it will be a relief for all the office staff when we're gone.

And a relief for me not to have to watch Pfeffer fiddling about anymore. He gets up. Sits down. Gets up. Sits down. He picks his nose and he rubs his chin. I wish I could cut his fingers off when I see it. I leave the table, even though I'm hungry. I'm always hungry. Only Pfeffer could make me walk away from food.

"Peter! Sit down!"

"Excuse me, I'm not hungry."

"Don't be rude!"

I sit down. It's not me who's rude. It's not me with my finger up my nose at the table. I look down so I can't see him.

"I can't bear it when children sulk," he says. I sigh. Margot sends me a glance of pure pity. Anne just looks relieved that it's not her in trouble for a change.

I think of my friend Hans. I haven't thought about him for ages. I wish he was here. Why did the Franks have to have just girls? If Margot was a boy we could play catch in the attic. Hans would know what I mean about Pfeffer. I wish it was him sitting opposite me, not Margot. I wonder where he is now. No I don't. No I don't. We used to joke that we both looked so German we could join the Hitler Youth. Perhaps he's a spy? If I got out of here could I be a spy?

I could do it.

The thought fills me with excitement.

I could stand up right now and walk down the stairs and into the street.

What would happen? Maybe nothing.

"Please may I leave the table?"

"Yes," Mutti says quickly, before anyone else can say anything. Mrs. Frank gives a sharp snort of disapproval. I go into my room. I can still hear them all, of course. They're right next door. I lie on the bed and pretend I'm a spy. I infiltrate the Nazi intelligence and blow up the labor exchange.

It feels good.

Until I have to get up and start French and English homework.

In French they don't say I love you; they say, *Je t'adore.*

Italian: *Te amo.*

German: *Ich liebe dich.*

Dutch: *Ik hou van jou.*

Anne and Margot could probably tell you how to say it in Latin and Greek, and write it in shorthand too! Well, good luck to them. How often do you fall in love with an ancient Roman or a Greek god?

If I ever get out of here I'm going to make love in so many languages—to a girl from every nation (except Germany). Or if I find Liese, I'll make love to just one girl in every language.

I have a list of things to do if I ever get out of here.

I'll make money.

I'll eat whatever I want.

Wear different clothes every day.

Buy a trilby.

I won't be a Jew, or a Christian or anything; I'll just be a man.

I'll make furniture. I'll swim in the sea. I'll have cats. I'll live. I'll never see Pfeffer or the Franks again. But right at this very moment I have to study commercial English. It is so boring. Shipments. Trainloads. Here's my letter.

Dear Sir/Madam,

I am pleased to inform you that we have your requirement of one shipload of prophylactics, as requested. These are for your newly freed Jews.

As you are aware, they are captive for years many now. And the need is quite high up, I believe. Please dispatch, forthwith, the said sum.

Yours faithfully,

Peter van Pels

I have to <u>underline the relevant business phrases</u>. I didn't give this letter to Mr. Frank to mark, even though it's quite good for me! Maybe I'll show it to Margot; maybe not.

I like to see her blush sometimes.

FEBRUARY 13, 1944 — PETER STRUGGLES
WITH DR. PFEFFER

Pfeffer is driving me mad. He can't sit still. We should have made it clear: Please do not come and live in such a small space if you are incapable of not moving. We're trying to listen to the radio, he's up and down and fiddling with the reception, pretending to make it better until I can't bear it.

"Please, can't you just stop?" I mutter.

"I'll be the judge of when I stop!" he says.

"A poor judge!" The words come out before I know it. I blush.

"Yes, Fritz, sit down and allow us all to listen in peace!" says Father. Mutti sends him a glance of approval. I look at the floor.

FEBRUARY 14, 1944 — ANNE AND PETER
ARE IN THE ATTIC TOGETHER

I'm lying in a patch of sunlight in the attic. It's cold; cold and dusty all around me. On my left the clothes are drying. Sometimes I swap them around, just for fun. I put Mutti's big knickers next to Mr. Frank's underwear. It makes me smile. It makes Mutti so cross when the washing gets mixed up.

I concentrate on the sun on my face. I try to forget that it's not really summer. I pretend we still live on Zuider-Amstellaan near Merwedeplein and that I'm on a day trip to the beach. I can hear the waves beside me; feel the sand beneath me. The open sky and air are all around me. Soon, I'll sit up and we'll have a picnic, and when I get back we'll all go to Oasis, the ice cream parlor where all us kids used to go. Anne was always there; she could have been bought ice creams every day for a year! Everybody loved her. Other times I'm on the beach at Zaandvoort and sometimes I'm just floating in the sea.

Weightless.

Anne and Margot sometimes pretend they're on the flat roof at Merwedeplein. Anne says she's with her grandmother. Margot, as usual, says nothing, but thinks a lot. I look at them both sometimes, with their heads so close together that their hair tangles. But today it's just me.

"Peter?"

I didn't notice Anne in the corner, searching through a box of books.

She's so quiet I didn't hear a thing. Anne isn't so clumsy these days. There was a time when she couldn't make it through a room without banging into something or knocking it over.

"Mmm?" I say.

I open my eyes. Just a bit. Above me the chestnut tree is golden in the light. The sun's a halo around its brown branches. In autumn the leaves are as gold as coins. Or brown—and sometimes, but not often—there's a red leaf. They fall off the tree in shoals.

"I wish I could do that," I whisper.

"What?" Anne says.

"Float away, like leaves."

I feel her head arrive on the floor next to mine. She has to put it there. The patch of sunlight's only small.

"But then they all die, silly!" she says. I close my eyes. I don't answer. The sunlight's so glorious after winter. Wonderful. We just lie there—it's nice. I wish we could float away like this in the sun. Like leaves. But we can't—and it's only February, and so even with each other's body warmth it's too cold to lie still for long. We sit up.

"I hate Pfeffer sometimes," I hear myself say. She smiles at me.

"He's not that bad, just irritating." She smiles.

"I didn't mean to be so rude yesterday, I just . . . Sometimes the wrong words come out and I just . . ."

"I know."

"You don't, you're never at a loss for what to say."

"Which is why I sometimes say too much."

"Sometimes I wish I could punch him! Why don't you tell him, Anne, at least he might listen then?" But Anne just laughs.

"Peter," she begins, "do you really think . . ." But I don't want any more questions. I'm sick of them. I just want a moment without them. I just want the sky and the tree and the feel of the sunlight on my face. So I raise my hand to her lips, and touch her mouth with the tip of my finger. Her eyes widen. Her lips feel soft, but dry—flaky beneath my fingers. Her eyes go very still. I take my finger away and she smiles.

And for once she doesn't say a word.

We watch the patch of sunlight crawl up the wall and disappear. She puts her head on my shoulder. And I put my arm around her. She is thin, like cat bones. We sit together for a while.

And it's nice.

It's not good to remember such things here in the camp. We're sometimes five in a bunk. But there's no warmth. We are alone. Each alone. Each in a fight against chance to last one more hour. One more day. One more night. One more life. We do it by standing on others. We do it by standing together. But in the end, each man does it alone.

What else is possible when death waits?

FEBRUARY 16, 1944 — MARGOT'S BIRTHDAY

In the morning I go and give Margot her present. It's a door-stop. It's meant to be a joke. I mean, we never need to keep doors open, we need more time with them closed. She closes her eyes and smiles.

"Thanks, Peter!"

"That's all right, I hope . . . well, I mean . . ."

"That I'll need it one day?" she says gently.

"Yes!" I say with relief. Margot always seems to know what I mean.

Anne is in and out of my room all day, needing to go up to the attic. First it's for coffee and then it's for potatoes.

"I'm spoiling Margot!" she says. "What else have I to give her but my labor?" I get up quickly and move my papers from the attic steps. Hide the drawings. It's taken me a while to get it, but now I'm sure. Anne's decided to fall in love with me. It was Margot who gave me the clue.

"Anne keeps coming into my room," I told her.

"Oh!" said Margot. "She's probably being Deanna Durbin in a sports car desperately hoping yet another man won't fall in love with her!" And she held her hand over her mouth. "That was unkind," she said. "Sorry."

"No," I tell her. "That explains it." And it does. Poor Anne, sitting in a cramped room with Peter van Pels wishing she was a film star!

I have no illusions. If we weren't stuck in the Annex, Anne Frank wouldn't look twice at me. I remember her eleventh birthday. I was thirteen. I gave her some chocolate, and even as she said thank you she was looking over my shoulder to see who was coming through the door. I don't know what to do about it.

It was nice that time in the attic, holding each other . . . and it's nice to have someone to chat to. But . . . there's only one problem. Me. I'm not sure I want to be Anne's substitute lover!

"Shall I close the trap door?" she asks on her way up the steps.

I shake my head. "I'll do it. Just knock when you want to come down."

I think she's hoping I might offer to go up there with her, but I can't.

I don't know what to do.

She spends a good ten minutes up in the attic. She must be freezing.

Is she hoping I'll go up there?

I don't know.

I sit and wait for her to come down.

"Oh," she says airily, "it took me ages. I couldn't find any small ones." I take the pan off her and look. The potatoes are all the size of eggs. They're tiny! I smile at her. She's shivering. I don't know what to say.

"They all look fine to me," I manage, but for the look of hope in her eyes I don't have any words at all.

I wish I could say, "It's all right. Don't worry. I know how it feels to want someone to love. I know what it's like to long for it." But I don't say anything. I just look at her, and then she's gone.

When she comes back again I can't bear it. I try to stop her. I offer to go up to the attic and get the potatoes for her. We argue. She wins. I let her go. I sit down at my desk and put my head in my hands. I look at the steep steps, knowing she's up there waiting.

I won't go up. I can't. I don't want to.

"Can I look at your work?" she asks when she finally comes down. She flicks her hair back, tilts her head on one side and gives me a film-star smile. I smile back. She sits on the bed. I stay by the desk.

I talk. I talk to her about nothing at all: about the way things were at home, the garden, Mutti's meals. It's strange. She draws the words out of me. They grow. I talk about the war. I even tell her how I think Russia and England will end up enemies one day—they have to, they're so different.

"And us Jews, everyone thinks we're different, and we are," she says.

The words come out before I think: "But we don't have to be."

"But, what do you mean?" She sounds so horrified I blush again. I talk about how hopeless I am, how useless with words—and then somehow I try again.

"But we could be anything, couldn't we? I mean I could have been born a Christian," I say.

"Would you want to be?" she asks.

"No! It's not that. I don't mean that. It's more that, well, why be anything?"

She looks horrified. "Then where would you belong?" she asks. "What are we fighting for if we're all the same?"

"We wouldn't all be the same! We're both Jews and we're not the same, are we? Anyway, I don't see that it's important that anyone knows whether I'm Jewish or not, at least not after the war."

"But why would you lie?" she cries.

"It's not lying it's . . ." But it's not like thinking out things for myself, or talking to Mouschi. I can't explain. I run out of words.

"Oh, the Jews will always be the *chosen* people," I say, angry.

"Well, it would be nice if for once we were chosen for something good!"

She laughs, and the moment is over. She goes on talking and it's nice, listening to her voice. Like listening to the sea, whispering over the sand at Zaandvoort.

"Are you afraid, Peter?" she asks suddenly. I think about it. Am I? Am I afraid? Sometimes I am. I was afraid at the break-in. But mostly I'm not afraid. Not of that. I'm more afraid I won't ever understand how this happened—or why. Mostly I'm afraid of me. Of the thoughts I have and not knowing what to do with them. And so that's what I say.

But what do I know?

I was right to be afraid. I was right. We should all fear knowing ourselves.

Lovers know; they learn it the easy way. We learned it the hard way—the knowledge that our bodies are stronger than our minds. That our bodies will fight to the death for the life within them, whatever we like to think of ourselves.

FEBRUARY 17, 1944 — ANNE IS IN THE VAN PELSES' ROOM, AND MAKES HER FEELINGS CLEAR

Anne is always up in our rooms now. I can hear her next door, reading to Mutti. I can hear the hum of her voice, but not the words. I like the sound of her voice when she reads.

"Amazing!" says Mutti when she's finished. "And you really thought all that up yourself? Or was it a real dream you had?"

"Well," says Anne, "you see, it's what's called a personification. In Greek tales they make trees and rivers and all things into gods, but I've just made them into ideas! So in 'Eve's Dream' the rose is arrogance and the bluebell is modesty!"

"And what have you done with us, Miss Minx?" asks Mutti. Anne starts to read again. This time Mutti laughs out loud and Anne stops too and giggles. I wonder what it's about. "So in this story we van Pelses are the stomachs and you Franks are brains!" says Mutti.

"Oh!" says Anne. "I didn't mean . . ." I go into the room.

"I like hearing you read," I say.

This time it's her blushing. "Hang on!" she says and runs downstairs. Mutti raises her eyebrows at me. Anne's up again in a second. We go into my room.

"Listen to this!" She begins to read. She reads the words so gently and clearly that somehow I can tell they're her words. That it's her making the story happen. I rest my head on the desk and listen. She's talking of a girl, a girl like her, who is sitting on a bench in a garden. A boy comes past. Slowly I feel my face redden beneath my arms. I'm glad my head is hidden. The boy is seventeen. The boy and the girl begin to talk. The words ring in my head:

"Do I look as though people would be afraid to talk to me?" says the girl.

"Well, not now that I see you better!" says the boy.

She's writing about us. The boy in the story is me—or at least I think he is. She goes on reading. Actions, words, things I've said—things she's said, things we've done. They're all jumbled, mixed up together and turned into the words she's reading. I don't know what to do, or what to say. I keep my head down. I go on listening. The boy and girl are talking about God. The questions, the doubts, they're mine. The answers and the conviction, they're Anne's. It's all there written down. Thank God I didn't tell her my real doubts. About God himself.

"Peter?" she asks, and I realize she's stopped reading, that she's waiting for me to say something. I raise my head. What can I say? Can I tell her the truth—that I feel stolen?

"Perhaps God is a personification, too," I suggest, but she

147

isn't listening. Her eyes are wide and shining, waiting for something more. We stare at each other. There's nowhere else to look. I don't know what she wants or what to say, except: "I wish you hadn't done that. I wish you hadn't put me in a story and made me feel like nothing I say is safe with you anymore." I can't say that, not when she's looking at me with such hope in her eyes, waiting to hear how good it is.

Mutti appears in the doorway. "So many ideas!" she says. "I'm surprised your hair doesn't all fall out! No wonder it's so curly!" I look at her, grateful, and she winks at me.

"I just wanted you to see," says Anne, her eyes never leaving mine, "that I don't just write to be funny. I can be serious too!"

I nod. But I don't like how it's made me feel, like anyone could flick a page and pull me out. Anyone could know what she thinks about me without ever guessing what I really think at all. I can't say anything. Anne doesn't notice, or does she? I'm not sure. All I know is that she smiles and leaves.

Which is a relief.

FEBRUARY 23, 1944 — ANNE AND PETER
SPEND TIME TOGETHER

The sun's shining. Every morning I go up the stairs to the attic and sit in it. Most mornings Anne comes too. We sit in a
patch of sunshine. I like it like this best. Quiet. Silent. Just
enjoying what's here. Perhaps if I hadn't been stuck in the
Annex I would never have noticed how wonderful a tree, just
one tree, can be. Or a patch of sunshine. Or the glitter of
raindrops on a branch. But that doesn't change the fact that
when I get out of here I'm going to paint whole landscapes,
wide seas, horizons that go on forever!

I stretch, get up, and start chopping wood for the stove.
Anne follows. I think, *Oh no! She'll start talking again.* But
she doesn't. She stays quiet and watches as I chop—so quiet
that I forget she's there after a while.

I love chopping wood. I love the concentration. I like
taking in the grain, working out where to strike, measuring
it with my eyes and hitting it just right. Full on, or at an an-
gle, whatever will break the log the right way. I like the swing
of the ax. Sometimes, when I'm alone, I imagine I'm hack-
ing our enemies into little tiny pieces. It feels good. I sigh.
When I'm finished I look up and smile, remembering she's
there.

"Sometimes," I say, "I imagine I'm in a forest, outside a hut, chopping."

She smiles and we both look out the window, all the way over the city to the sea. The air is clear and cold. I imagine it on my face. I sigh and close my eyes for just a moment.

"Wonderful!" I say quietly. Anne nods. I'm surprised. Surprised that she can speak without words.

And be content.

FEBRUARY 26, 1944 — MR. FRANK
IS CONCERNED

"Oh, but the weather's so beautiful. Please, Daddy!" says Anne.

"No, Anne." His voice is gentle, but if I were Anne I wouldn't bother to argue. He means it. She pouts and narrows her eyes.

"Please?" she asks again.

He smiles. "No," he says back.

"Why not?" she hisses.

"Because even though the sun shines, even though we don't feel like it, the work must be done."

"But I do it every day. Even here, even though there's probably no point!" she says.

"Anne!" hisses her mother, but Mr. Frank just carries on, quietly.

"Especially then. Especially when there is no point, because that is when we need something to hold on to," he says. "So go on now. Sit down and do your work."

Anne gives a big sigh, turns away, and stomps downstairs to her own room. She doesn't see her parents smile at each other.

"I must see if I can make our clothes hang together for just a little longer," says Mrs. Frank. Mr. Frank pats her on the shoulder. "What would we do without you, Edith?" he whispers. And she smiles. I can see how much his praise means to her. I think it must be nice to have someone feel like that about you. That your thoughts matter.

I go into my room. I want to draw Mr. Frank. I've wanted to for a long time, but somehow I don't have the courage. I'm not sure I can get him right. I think that maybe if I lie down on the bed for a while and picture him, then it might come to me—the right way to do his face.

"Peter?"

I open my eyes and he's there. I sit up quickly. I can see he doesn't think much of me dozing the day away.

"Yes," I say, "I was just . . ."

"I'm sorry to disturb you, do you mind if we talk?" I shake my head. I notice he has closed the door. I notice it's quiet outside. I notice that no one can hear us. I wonder what it is about.

No I don't.

I know what it is about.

"Anne," he says. I nod. His face is kind. His eyes are dark and curious like Anne's.

"We find ourselves in a difficult situation, wouldn't you

say, Peter?" he begins, and then he waits. I don't say anything. I don't know what to say.

"Anne's very young," he says after a while, "and very determined!" That makes me smile. He smiles back.

"I would never . . ." I begin, but he holds up his hand.

"I'm not here to accuse either of you," he says gently. "I'm here to talk, to think." I nod again. "I suppose," he goes on, "that the problem is that within these walls you young people have so few choices." I nod again. There's not much more I *can* do.

"But it's not only Anne that's here, Peter. You see there's Margot too, and she . . ." He sighs, "she would never, well, make quite as much of an effort to be noticed, shall we say, as Anne does."

I nod again.

"Two girls, but only one of you."

I smile and blush.

"So what will you do?"

I'm not sure if he's really asking me the question, or whether he's talking to himself.

"I don't know," I say.

"Well, perhaps we should think about it?"

"I . . . sir . . . Mr. Frank . . . I think Margot thinks of me more as a brother."

"Mmm, if you know what Margot is thinking, Peter, then you know far more than any of the rest of us do."

We don't say anything for a while. I wonder whether I should mention how desperate Anne is to know more about men's bodies, or how wonderful it is to sit in the attic together in a patch of sunlight. I wonder if Mr. Frank ever felt worried that he might never make love to a girl. I wonder how they all find it so easy to put these things into words. Just the thought of trying makes me start to blush and stammer. So I don't say anything at all.

"And Anne?" he asks.

"Anne wants to be adored!" I blurt out. "And I'm the only one here."

He laughs.

"Oh, I know Anne wouldn't even notice me out of here," I say.

"Peter, you have no vanity at all; a wonderful trait in a person!"

"Thank you!" Now I really *am* blushing.

"Mr. Frank?"

"Yes?"

"Thank you for hiding us." The words come out very formally. "I would never do anything to . . . to make you sorry."

He pats my shoulder. "I know that you wouldn't *intend* to,

Peter, but I also know that our bodies can be stronger than our intentions at your age. Anne is only fourteen, even though she has always believed herself to be older than she is. And, Peter, she isn't always kind."

"I . . . don't . . ."

"Well, I'm afraid she might be unable to resist crowing over her conquest, to Margot. And they have missed out on so much, both of them. For Margot to have to manage that too . . . , well . . ."

"It's complicated," I say, and it is; my head's spinning.

"Yes," he agrees.

"I think it's best if all three of you are friends," he says finally. I nod.

"I'm trying to think of you too, Peter."

I nod again. "Mr. Frank?"

"Yes?"

"Will you still be a Jew after the war?" He stops and looks at me.

"Well," he says after a while, "it would certainly be nice to think that we might have that choice!" And he disappears down the stairs.

It's a long time before I realize that he hasn't answered my question.

Mr. Frank is probably right. We should see less of each other, but it's not that easy. The problem is the words. They're addictive. Perhaps if Mutti knew how it feels she'd warn me like she warns Papi about his cigarettes. Speaking, gossiping, it's infectious. Last night we spent forever talking about Pfeffer—*again*—and why we hate him so much.

"He fiddles!"

"I know."

"The way he's always touching things before moving them. Ugh!"

"The way he's always right!"

"That dimple in his chin—I'd like to stick a pin in it."

"When he's talking it makes me want to scratch, like a flea. I have to get out!"

"Do you remember when Mouschi had fleas?"

"He spends fifteen whole minutes praying! Sometimes I even have to look at his naked back. Ugh!"

The thought makes me sick. Anne giggles and imitates the noises he makes in the night. Snuffles, like an animal, soft puffs of air. Intimate. I stand up.

"Peter?" she asks, tucking her head to one side.

"It's disgusting," I say, "that you have to share a room with him."

Her arms are wrapped around her legs and she shrugs her shoulders. "Why?" she asks. I smile at her. She's like Mouschi waiting to be stroked. Waiting for the right touch, the right words.

"You're not a child!" I say.

"Aren't I?" she asks back. She tosses her hair over her shoulder. *But she is a child,* I hear Mr. Frank say in my head. I realize she's done her hair again, pinned it up to look like the film stars on her wall. She's waiting. Looking up at me. Gleaming. I sit down beside her. I look at her and I say, "No. No, you aren't a child." She tips her head back and looks at me through lowered lashes.

I have to look away.

For a moment I can't meet her eyes.

Something inside me lurches.

When I look back again she's stopped posing, she's just Anne again.

"Peter?" she asks.

"It's nothing," I say, but that's not true. It's everything . . . It's Liese. It's the sound of her voice saying my name, the memory of her dancing in my dreams. The weight of her shaven head in my hands. The sound of clicking train wheels. It's all the things that can't be said, all the things that stop my eyes meeting Anne's.

She smiles. Perhaps she thinks that I'm overcome by her flirting. Her beauty. Her wit. Perhaps I am. I don't know. I only know that the sight of her hurts. And that I'd like to be alone. Or with Mouschi. Or anywhere except here and now—with Anne.

Anne and her eyes that are full of searching, full of longing, full of the hope that I can give them something back. That's what I can't bear. Her hope. It's like seeing someone naked. I don't think I can take the weight of it.

Her expectation.

"We should go down now." I try to say it gently, but her face falls. And then she finds the words to lift it.

"You're a very decent boy, Peter," she says. I hold out my hand and she stands. I open the trap door and shield her with my body as we go backwards down the steep steps. She turns to me at the bottom of the stairs. "Thank you," she says, as solemn as a lady. She turns to go. But then she stops at the door, makes a half-turn and smiles at me over her shoulder. A bright, studied smile. A smile that should be lit by a thousand cameras and broadcast across the world—a practiced smile.

It's a waste because there's only me here. And I don't know what to do with such a smile.

Am I good?

Am I decent?

I don't know.

I don't know anything anymore.

Memories are addictive too. They grow. Like frog spawn. They breed. Like rats. Like the Nazis imagined we bred. We stood before them, naked. Not naked like hope, but naked like loss. It's not only our clothes they took when they stripped us—it was our being. It must come, that bit of the story.

Tell me.

Please tell me.

Are you there?

Are you listening?

Will you turn away from me?

Or will you bear it—as I must?

FEBRUARY 29, 1944 — ANOTHER
BREAK-IN

Father's angry.

"Peter!"

"Yes?"

"What do you think you are doing, leaving a mess like that downstairs?"

"What?"

"Can't you even do the few things we ask of you properly?"

"I do!"

"You call leaving the office in that state reasonable? And with the doors open?"

"I didn't!"

"And now you lie! The front door is locked so who else could it be?"

"I don't know. All I know is that I helped Bep in the office and that we left it tidy!"

"Don't be sarcastic as well as idle!"

Mutti comes down from the attic with an armful of clean clothes.

"If Peter tells you he's done it, he's done it!" she says.

"And if logic tells you otherwise, you will still pretend to be blind!" he shouts back.

Quietly.

"In the case of my son I will be blind if I choose to. Couldn't you turn a blind eye too every now and then?"

"And open them to find what?" he hisses. "A room full of mess and maybe a girl full of mess too!"

"Hermann!"

"Father!"

"Well, I only say what everyone thinks. We aren't blind! That girl follows you around like a puppy. In my day the girls had some pride."

"What would you know about girls and pride?" Mutti hisses back as she folds the clothes, furiously. "Is there room for pride in love? Is there room for dreams within these walls? Do you have any feelings left at all except for cigarettes?"

"Ach! Would the world's problems be solved by a man giving up his last few smokes?"

"Maybe."

"Now you're being ridiculous!"

"And you? You aren't being ridiculous?"

I leave the room. They can go on like this for hours.

"See? One day you'll drive him away completely."

"Where to? Where will I drive him to, Auguste? There's nowhere to go to except next door, you silly woman!"

"Don't you call me silly! You with the sense of a . . . a . . . fly!"

I climb the steps to the attic and lean my head against the beams. The wood feels rough and comforting.

During supper Anne tries to catch my eye. Margot keeps her head down. Mr. Frank is watching all three of us. I leave as soon as I can. I pace in my room. Up and down. I stop at the window and breathe a little air. Finally I sit down and begin to draw. A picture of Mr. Frank. But no matter how hard I try, I can't get it right. His face slips away from me.

I try to sleep, but I'm too angry. I wake up early and wait for the dark to change to half-light. The thoughts go around in my head: *Why us, why do we have to be here? Why can't Papi just leave me alone? Why are they always arguing—and nearly always about me?*

In the end I get up and decide to go and see if there really is a mess in the office. I creep down in the half-dark. There's no sound. At times like this it's hard to believe there's really a war happening at all.

I feel air on my face. At first I don't realize what it is. I stand on the stairway very still and feel it all over me. A breeze. Not just on my face. Not just the sound of a breeze in the leaves of the chestnut tree—but air all over me. And then I realize what it means—the front door at the bottom of the stairs isn't locked, it must be open. Someone's been in the building. So that's what the mess in the office was—another burglary! I check the front office. Mr. Kugler's briefcase is gone, and a projector.

I run up the stairs and wake Mr. Frank. He sends me back down to lock the door. I'm scared now. What if someone is there? What if I can't resist the temptation raging inside me to look outside, or even stronger, the desire to stand in the street for a second—just one second? What difference could it make? I could see the whole street. All of it. Not just a sliver of it through the window. It's like longing for a decent meal, this longing for my eyes to see something whole.

To look up and see the sky.

I slam the door quickly and lock it. I stand behind it shaking. I lean against it. I hear footsteps go past. How far away were they? If I had done it, if I had stepped outside, would they have seen me? Are they German footsteps? Dutch? Would they have betrayed me, or pitied me? I can't know because they all sound the same—footsteps.

I head back upstairs.

Everyone's standing in the kitchen around the breakfast table. Except it isn't a kitchen yet because Mutti and Papi are still in bed.

"We're holding court!" says Papi, propped up on pillows. "Any questions for the king and queen?"

"Someone's been in the office!" says Anne. "They've stolen Mr. Kugler's briefcase and they might have heard us!"

"And your father has something to say to you, Peter," says Mutti.

"Obviously you did not make the mess downstairs," he says.

"And so?" says Mutti.

"And so I wrongly accused you."

"And you are?" asks Mutti.

"Not a child!" explodes Papi.

"Well then, say sorry and stop behaving like one!"

"It's all right," I say, "but why was the downstairs door still open?"

Everyone falls silent.

"They must have been disturbed by me going down there last night," says Papi.

"They know someone's hiding here then?" asks Anne, quietly. She looks white and scared. Margot puts her arm around her. "It's all right, silly, we're all still here."

"Anne," says Mr. Frank, quietly, "many people know we're here. We rely on them to feed us, to keep us safe."

"But nobody we trust would steal Mr. Kugler's briefcase."

"And how was the door locked last night?" I ask.

"It must be someone with a key," says Mr. Frank. "We

need to wait and find out more when the staff arrive. Until then let's try and eat something, shall we?"

Everyone looks at Mutti. She looks back. "Yes?" she says, smiling.

"Uh . . . well . . ." says Mr. Frank.

"Well, if you all vacate the room, I will get out of bed and make the breakfast everyone wants," she says. We all crowd into my room to wait. Dr. Pfeffer farts. Anne and Margot start to giggle.

"Really!" says Mrs. Frank.

"We're ready," calls Mutti, and we fall back into the room, taking great breaths. Anne's face is red from holding her breath. I catch her eye. We start to smile and then to laugh.

Quietly.

Mr. Frank stares at me. I look away.

"Really, Anne!" snaps Mrs. Frank in a whisper. "You should stop pestering Peter."

Anne stops. She stops dead. It's like her mother's thrown cold water in her face.

"Anne?" I ask, and she turns toward me, her face blank with pain. "Can you help me finish the crossword after breakfast? You know how hopeless I am at getting all the way to the end!"

She smiles again and tosses her hair, gives her mother a hard stare.

"Of course," she says. Mr. Frank raises an eyebrow at me.

"And you too, of course, Margot," I say. "Only please promise to let us *try* and work out the answers for ourselves." I can't see her eyes behind her glasses, but Margot smiles her sweet smile and lowers her head. I'm exhausted. I wish it was the weekend and that I could escape to the warehouse and sit with Boche for a while, but it's a weekday and we haven't even had breakfast yet. If you can call it breakfast: ersatz coffee and bread with a tiny pat of butter—and jam. As much jam as we want. We could shit jam; maybe that's what makes Pfeffer fart so much. Shame it doesn't smell of strawberries.

Outside the Annex there are footsteps, footsteps coming closer and stopping at the door. Outside the Annex someone is curious. Someone wonders. Someone has crept up the stairway and been into the office after hours. Someone has heard Papi muttering about the mess.

Someone thinks we're here.

Someone is going to find out.

LATER THAT DAY

It's evening before I can get away to the storeroom. I sit against the wall and close my eyes. I don't want to draw, or dig cork, I just want to be alone and think in the dark.

I nearly went outside.

I saw daylight.

We live in the dark. We've gotten used to it, but in summer going up to the attic is like being blinded. Our eyes are different now. We see more in the dark than we can in the light. Sometimes I think we'll go blind if we ever do get out. I don't know. But I know that we creep around in the dark. And disappear at the sight of light, just like the cockroaches they tell us we really are.

"Don't we, Mouschi?" I can feel Mouschi curling around my legs. He looks up. I hold out my hands and he lifts his head and sniffs, puts his head in my palm.

I'm grateful.

I want to feel something warm in my arms in the dark and have the smell of the barrels and the quiet all around me. You might say that's not manly. I don't mind. Not fighting is not manly. Sitting like a duck waiting to be shot is not manly. Not even having an escape route out of here, that's not manly. Dreaming of Liese and pretending my hands are her hands rather than doing the real thing, I suppose that's not manly. And that's the other thing about being here. All the things that make sense out there—they don't count in here. We're in a different game—our game is survival.

"Isn't it, Mouschi?" I stop walking up and down. I didn't even realize I was doing it. I'm pacing the whole length of the room, backwards and forward as Mouschi weaves in and out of my moving ankles.

I sit down and Mouschi curls up in my lap, begins his machine-like purr.

Survival.

It requires one thing more than any other, and that's your pride. I really think it's true. Mr. Frank stays proud because he believes it will all work out in the end. That we'll survive, somehow. I'm not so sure. At least not when I'm alone in the dark.

"Am I, Mouschi?" Mouschi purrs.

Sometimes I wonder if Mr. Frank ever looks out the window. The herd's getting smaller. There are less and less of us. We're like water swirling down the plughole—soon there'll be none of us left. The bath will be empty.

It makes no difference at all to them whether I *think* I am a Jew or not. Whether I believe, whether I practice or not. All that matters to them is that it's in my blood, even one speck of it is enough to infect all of me.

That's how they see it.

"Eh, Mouschi?" But Mouschi doesn't answer.

There's so much time here. Either you can get depressed and stay in bed forever—or you can get up. You can study. You can draw, or write or read. You can pretend there is a future waiting for you. But if you do that, then you have to face the questions that come with it. It's best to do this alone, believe me. Margot got that straightaway. She always keeps her thoughts to herself. I'm just too slow, so the chance to join in the conversation never comes for me. Everyone else gets there first! Anne wants everyone to listen to her questions, but all it does is stir us all up inside. And when that happens, everyone gets going. Which means we have to listen to the same old arguments. And then Mutti gets upset and goes red. Anne's mother goes cold and speaks like she's the oracle, while telling Anne off. Mr. Frank sighs and looks like he wishes he could knock everyone's heads together and then Papi tries to make it all better with one of his terrible old jokes.

So, really, it's best to keep quiet and keep your questions to yourself. There are so many. Will it ever end, and when it does will there be any of us left? If the Allies get close, will the Nazis kill us all? Are we meant to believe God chose us for this?

Why?

You see. I have no answers. I'm not clever like Anne or Margot or Liese. I'm slow, and I only have questions with no answers. I can't control my thoughts. I'm sure they're wrong somewhere, but that's what happens when you ask too many questions. You just make more and more inside of you.

Will we be imaginary one day? Will we be just like one of Anne's stories? Or worse, will the story that survives be the Nazi one—that we were only ever good enough to be wiped out?

How?

How could anybody do this?

MARCH 3, 1944 — PETER REMEMBERS

BEFORE

It's been snowing. I stand in the attic, waiting for Anne, and stare at the branches of the chestnut tree all covered in white. There are stars behind it. The night is a clear, strange blue. I know I could paint all my life. But I could never make a blue that dark. That deep. That beautiful. I could never make stars like little holes of light in the night. Even van Gogh couldn't do it. I remember the crunch of snow under my feet. I remember throwing snowballs. Sometimes the snow was so deep there was no school. Gangs of us stretched out around the green on Merwedeplein attacking each other with snowballs. Hiding behind the bushes and trees. Wet hair. Red cheeks. Air so cold it made shapes with our breath. I stare out of the attic window. I wish the bells would ring. Anne's right, how will we ever know we're free if there are no bells to ring? I would like to feel the snow on my face. It buries everything. It buries us. Maybe one day the world will thaw, and we will melt away from here?

Maybe.

Snow.

I will never be able to stand and stare at it and find it beautiful again!

The Auschwitz snow is terrible. It made us dance with cold. Use energy we didn't have. It made my breath burn against the holes in my teeth. We stood in it, in thin pajamas hour after hour, day after day. It never got easier. Each day was as dreadful as yesterday. There is no word for it, Auschwitz-cold.

And at the end of it: a hut, a beating, a thin soup, another day of not knowing if you will live or die.

The dread of a seleckcja.

Knowing that the command will come. Each morning. Invading your half-dreams, your half-sleep, pulling you back to the nightmare that's your life.

WYSTAWACH.

Wake up.

"But, Peter!" Anne says. She is happy. Her eyes are shining. "*You* think so? Don't you?"

"Think what?"

"That mother's wrong. I mean, she's always saying that we should manage by thinking about how much *worse* life is for everyone else."

"Sometimes it can help," I say quietly.

"Oh yes?" she says. "Well then, why are you always looking at the sky? Why do you chop wood as though it gives you such joy to do it just right?"

I smile.

"Don't just smile at me! Say something!" She's smiling too, though.

"What?" I say again. She throws a cushion at me.

"What, in case you don't know the fact, does not express an opinion, and why do I have to be locked up with the most irritating boy in the whole of Holland?" But she doesn't look irritated. I catch the cushion easily. No problem. Now we're both smiling.

"You talk too much. What does it matter what your mother does? Is she stopping you from enjoying the sky? She has her way, you have yours."

And I throw the cushion back. She doesn't reach for it. She lets it hit her in the face and falls back onto the attic floor.

"Anne?" She doesn't move. I know I haven't thrown it hard enough to hurt her, but still. "Anne?" I move toward her and gently take it off her face. She's smiling. She smiles a lot now. Most of all when she's with me. I like that. She makes an action like zipping up her smiling mouth. I laugh. Quietly.

I reach out a hand to help her up. She takes it. We sit together and look out the window. The sky is blue and beautiful. The sun is out. There are tiny buds on the chestnut tree, beneath the snow. Anne sighs deeply, and rests her head on my shoulder. I close my eyes. I smell her hair. I notice I haven't let go of her hand. It's small and neat inside mine. It's cold. She is always cold. I put my other hand over it. *I want to make it warm, that's all,* I say to Mr. Frank in my mind. *I just want her to be warm.* We sit there for a while looking out the window.

"But, Anne, you know," I say after a while, "there is suffering out there. No Jews on the street. No food. Death camps. I mean, perhaps your mother is right—things are worse for others."

"But we're here too." She sighs, dreamily, and her body rests deeper against mine. "We're still here, aren't we? Even if only this little piece of attic sky can see us. We are here and . . ." She stops and looks at me.

And there is so much I wish I could say. I think she's like
the gulls we see that flash silver across the sky. And I'm like
the chestnut tree that takes a whole six months just to put
out a single leaf. I sigh, because she's right, it is wonderful sometimes to be exactly where you are. Like in this
moment.

Right now.

And to forget the rest.

But I can't say all my thoughts. I never have been able to.
And so I just whisper her name instead. Anne. And she looks
at me. We stare at each other, and outside the sky and the
tree watch over us. And we are all waiting.

Waiting.

And wondering what will happen.

MARCH 22, 1944 — PETER THINKS
ABOUT ANNE

Anne is hard and bright and honest, but inside she is full of longing—the way I sometimes long for Liese, but have to hold Mouschi instead.

Is it so wrong to want to hold Anne?

Is it wrong to feel so glad that I can make her happy?

Well, is it?

I don't know.

Sometimes I still go up to the attic and listen to the gunfire in the night. There are planes overhead. It doesn't scare me anymore. I don't know why. I think that maybe it's because I know that nothing can stop what will happen. If we are hit we are hit. If the building catches fire, it catches fire and we'll be driven out of it. Exposed. I wonder if I will try to pretend to be German. Pretend? What do I *mean*? I am German, aren't I? That's how crazy everything is. That's how hard it is to work out even the simplest things these days.

———

Bep came up. She coughed as she told us about the airmen. She's thin. We're all thin. We don't get enough to eat. No one does. Everyone is ill. She told us how the Nazis sprayed the

178

airmen with bullets as they floated down from the sky.
Mr. Frank shook his head and said it was very different in
his day.

"There's not enough food," said Mutti. "Not for anyone.
They don't want to feed them, that's why they shot them!"

"It's not always about food, Auguste!" said Mrs. Frank.

They begin to argue. Mrs. Frank stabs at our clothes with
her needle. In, out, in, out, in time with her words. Mutti goes
red. I go to my room. I can still hear their voices, arguing.

"Sorry," I whisper to the dead airmen. Bep didn't say that
they're dead, but I suppose they are. If I knew I would die
tomorrow, would I ask Anne for a kiss? For more than a kiss?
If she knew this was our last day ever, would she say yes?
Would it matter that we only kissed because we knew we
might be dead tomorrow?

Is that the only reason we want to?

I don't know.

How do you ever know, anyway?

———

Anne comes into my room quietly.

She twists her hands in front of her, nervous. I know I've
been mean to her, trying to stay away from her. It makes my
heart twist. It's horrible pushing her away when she's trying
so hard; like kicking a wingless bird.

"Can we go to the attic?" she asks. I nod. I go up first, open the trap door and then help her through. When we first came to the Annex we inched our way up the steps slowly, they're so steep. Now we can almost run up them. We sit on the cushions.

"Are you angry with me, Peter?" she asks. I don't know what to say, or how to say it. I am angry, but not with Anne. I'm angry we're stuck in the Annex, angry we're having to do this with everyone watching us, angry it's so obvious her mother doesn't approve of me and that her father's frightened for Margot.

"It's lots of things!" I blurt out.

"Is Mummy right? Am I pestering you?" she asks, and her voice is sharp, not with anger, but with needing to know. That's the way it is with Anne, always needing to know, whatever the truth is. I smile.

"It's not funny!" she says.

"Listen," I say, "just listen." She waits. I wait. I wait to know what to say. It takes a long time. I blush. The birds sing. A noisy truck goes past far below. I get up and shut the trap door, even though we'd hear anyone trying to come up.

"It's everything, Anne. Being stuck here, not knowing, wondering . . ." I stop. She waits. "I mean, what if this is it? What if this is the rest of our life? Or if we're found, what happens next? Why don't we have an escape route . . . and what if this is our only chance to . . . ?" She's quiet, so quiet it makes it difficult to go on. "To fall in love or to know each other . . ." I run out of words. I've said too much. I stop. I'm blushing. Anne's staring at me seriously, waiting.

"What do you think?" I ask.

"I'm not sure what you're saying," she says, but she's shaking.

"Anne! What if we never get out of here?"

"Don't!" The word comes out of her, short and desperate. "Please, Peter, don't!" She begins to shake uncontrollably. I reach for her.

"Oh, I'm sorry! I'm sorry, Anne." What have I done?

"It's just that . . ." She tries to speak but her voice is too shaky. "It's just that I've got so many things inside me. So much I need to do—and I've got to survive, Peter. *We've* got to!"

"We will, we will," I whisper, horrified. "Don't worry, Anne, your father will get us there. If anyone can, he can."

I hold her as tight as I can. I hold her as though I could stop this feeling, this fear from spilling out and drowning us. After a while the shakes become shudders.

"Sorry," she whispers.

"Don't be sorry," I whisper back. She takes a deep breath.

"I'm scared," she says. "Scared that all the things inside me will never see daylight."

"I know." I rock her. "Me too."

"What"—she hiccups—"what frightens you most? I mean the things you might not get to do," she whispers, looking up at me.

I look away from her. I can't say it—or can I? Can we really tell each other all the things inside us? Is it possible?

I don't know how.

"No, you tell me what you want to do," I whisper.

She doesn't hesitate, not for a second. The words tumble from her lips as though she already feels there's no time left to speak them.

"It's the stories," she says. "There are so many of them, Peter. Do you ever think how many there are? How many of us there might be, each with a story—and the ideas. Sometimes I think even a whole lifetime would never be enough to tell them . . ." She grasps my arm. Her grip's passionate and strong. "But I asked about you," she laughs.

I swallow.

"Peter?"

I take a deep breath.

"Peter?" she asks softly. "There must be something."

"I'm scared I'll never make love to a girl," I say quietly.

The words fall between us, softly, lightly. I feel her hand draw back.

"Oh!" she says. And she sits up, away from me. Her eyes grow as big as her face. Her mouth moves but nothing comes out. And then she covers her face with her hands and begins to laugh. Her whole body shakes.

"That's so . . . I . . ." she chokes the words. "I never imagined . . . I had no idea. That you would say that!"

"Neither did I!"

And then we can't speak because we're both laughing. She takes deep breaths and wipes the tears from her eyes.

"Anne?" I ask after a while.

"Yes?" she says.

"Don't put this in your diary."

"Why not?"

"I don't know."

"All right," she says quickly, "I won't."

We talk. We talk until the light fades and is gone. We talk until our words feel like they have a life of their own, that they stand out separate from us on the attic air.

"Anne," I say, "I know you would never have noticed me, if we weren't stuck in here."

She laughs and reaches for my hand.

"Oh, Peter!" she says. "And I might never have noticed

how amazing a single tree is, or a glimpse of the sky. I would be a different person. Probably a worse one! I'm not always proud of who I was, Peter."

"You're incredible!"

"So are you!"

"Anne?"

"Yes."

"There was a girl, on the outside. A girl called Liese."

"Liese Lieberman?"

It's hard hearing her name said out loud by some-one else.

"How about you?"

"There was a boy called Peter, Peter Schiff."

We're silent. We sit in the dark and hold each other's hands. We don't know what's happening to Liese or Peter. We don't know whether they're alive or dead. We only know that they're alive inside us—and that it hurts.

When we stand up to go down, I kiss the top of Anne's head. She squeezes my hand tight. We don't say any more. We don't need to, we both know that we're here, and they're not.

MARCH 26, 1944 — PETER IS FULL OF FEELINGS

She's opened a gate. The feelings flood through. I want to say: "My name is Peter van Pels. I am here. I am real, not just an idea. What would you do if I held you in my arms, Anne Frank, and kissed you?"

But I know I mustn't. I must think of Mr. Frank—and Margot. I take a deep breath and concentrate on what she's saying.

"I'm not going to be a *hausfrau!*" she says. I laugh. Anne could never be a *hausfrau*. She's too clumsy for one. She'd write a story and forget to cook supper. Have an idea. Forget to shop.

"You couldn't be a *hausfrau* if you tried."

"I could," she says haughtily. "I just don't want to be."

"Well," I laugh, "you'd better find a husband who won't mind."

"Perhaps I won't have a husband."

"Really?"

She gives me one of her wicked glances, holds a pretend cigarette in her hand, takes a long slow puff, and pulls it airily out of her mouth, her hand floating to her side.

"Do you really think it's necessary?" she drawls. "I mean in this day and age?"

I smile. There's so much I want to say to her.

"Yes, it is, if you want to have children."

She drops the pose and stares into the distance, then glances at me quickly.

"Perhaps I won't!" she says, defiantly. "I mean it's not obligatory, is it?"

"No," I say.

"I can't imagine children coming out of me," she says suddenly, "only stories."

I don't know what to say to that, so I don't say anything.

"Do you think that's dreadful?" she asks.

I shrug. "Why should it be? After this we should be able to do whatever we want to."

"I want to write, Peter!"

"You do write already," I say. She comes and sits beside me. Takes my hands.

"But will I ever write anything great?" she asks. "Something that's first-class, that changes people's lives?"

"Why not?" I say, because when Anne's like this it feels like she can do anything, think anything, be anyone. Sometimes. Sometimes the thought comes that I could be there with her, in the background. Like I am here. I think I might like it. I could check the doors. Keep her safe. I put my arm around her. We lie on the floor and her dreams pour over us. They are always there—over there. Somewhere else. In the future.

She can't see that I'm beginning to *like* it here. Because of her. She's changing everything. I look forward to coming up here and lying in the sun. Listening to her. Hearing the breeze through the tree. Opening my eyes. Seeing the glint of a gull in the sky. Wishing it could stay like this forever.

I like it.

But Anne wants more.

Not from me.

From the world.

"Have you ever kissed someone?" she asks suddenly. We both stare up at the beams of the attic roof.

"No," I say. I remember the feel of Liese's skin, the taste of the back of her hand as I kissed it goodbye. Soft. Warm.

"Me neither," says Anne. She sits up. Runs her tongue across her lips and presses them together. I smile up at her. At her anxious, determined face.

"I don't think that's how it is," I say. "I mean, when it happens it just happens, doesn't it?"

But maybe this *is* how it is. Perhaps for us, there is no time to wait and see. Perhaps for us there's no choice.

There's only here.

There's only now.

There's only Anne—who wants to know what it is to be kissed, and me—who'd like to make love to a girl.

She would prefer a film star, or at least someone clever. I would prefer Liese.

But they're not here.

And we are.

I sit up. I can't do it, not like this.

"We should go down now," I say.

And do I imagine it, or is she relieved?

Or maybe it's disappointment?

I don't know.

Does *she?*

If I had my time again? If she sat there like that, full of questions, full of longing? If I knew what I know now? Would I have done anything different? Because we had less time than we imagined.

Far less.

MARCH 27, 1944 — ANNE AND PETER ARE TOGETHER IN THE ATTIC

I love making Anne smile. I can do it by winking at her. I can do it by asking how she is or whether she wants to come to the attic. I'm doing it all the time at the moment because I'm trying to draw her and can't get her dimples to come out right. I never really noticed her face. How brown her eyes are, how sharp her face is—like her brain, clever and cutting. She knows and thinks so much, but she doesn't always know about people.

Everyone in the Annex has a new topic of conversation. Us.

"Anne's second home," says Pfeffer as she heads into my room. "Don't forget to come back to us, Anne!"

Anne smiles and winks, and acts like it's all completely normal. She's enjoying it, just like Mr. Frank said she would. As usual, I say nothing—but inside I'm raging. I hate it. What has any of it to do with them? Did they have to explain themselves to *their* parents? Can't they at least pretend that we have some privacy?

MARCH 29, 1944 — EVERYONE REALIZES
ANNE'S DIARY IS GOLD DUST

Last night government minister Mr. Gerrit Bolkestein announced on the radio that the writings of all those in hiding are to be gathered together after the war as testimony. Suddenly the whole Annex is talking about Anne's diary. Everyone wants to know what's in it. Everyone wants her to write about them. Mr. Frank talks about bearing witness. Mrs. Frank about testament. Papi retells his favorite jokes, just in case she's already forgotten them! Everyone thinks it's wonderful. Everyone except me—and Margot.

Margot says nothing.

"What if I don't want to be in it?" I ask at dinner (stinking kale and potatoes), because I don't.

"Quick, write that down, Anne!" says Papi, and everyone laughs. But I wonder. I wonder if they realize how passionate she is, how much it means to her. I shudder. This could change everything. Already Anne's staring at them as they speak. I try to catch her eye, but she's looking intently at Margot, waiting for a reaction.

"That's wonderful," says Margot, sweetly, but she breathes in deeply as she says it.

"We must give you more time to work on it," says Mrs. Frank. Anne looks amazed.

"Not in *my* room. I can't have Anne using any more time in my room. It's just not right to encourage her too much," says Dr. Pfeffer.

"It's absolutely not a problem, Pfeffer; Anne will have time in *our* room. It won't affect you at all," says Mr. Frank.

Margot closes her eyes. So where will she go, then? Nobody asks her, and she doesn't ask anybody.

Anne smiles. "Thank you, Daddy!" Mrs. Frank nods approval. "And you, Mummy!" But no one thanks Margot.

I can already imagine how Anne might see us. Mutti is a silly, fat flirt; Margot an irritating, perfect daughter; and me—who am I? The thought scares me. Especially when I think of everything I've told her.

MARCH 30, 1944 — PETER WATCHES
ANNE WRITE

I wait in the attic for her, but she doesn't come. I go down to the Franks' room; she's not in the sitting room so I knock on the bedroom door. "Oh, just go in," says Margot. "She never hears anything when she's writing." I open the door. Anne is sitting at the desk, her head is down and her fingers fly across the pages. She doesn't look up—she doesn't even know I'm here.

"Anne?" She jumps and stares up at me, her eyes furious and lost. She stares, and then she says my name.

"Peter?"

"We, uh, we said we'd meet, in the attic."

"Oh!" she says. For a moment it's like she's not here. She looks frightening, angry.

"It's fine," I whisper. "Later."

"There might not be a later!" she hisses, and turns back to the desk. She doesn't notice me leave. I close the door and stand there for a while, stunned.

Margot looks up from her book. "Impressive, isn't it?" she says drily. I nod, and leave.

Later, when Anne and I meet in the attic, we don't mention it, either of us. It's a secret thing, like being hidden.

We meet at night now, because her days are so full—we meet in the attic. We can't have candles, so we sit in the dusk and the dark.

"I spied on you," she says, "the other day, when you were in the storeroom with Boche."

"Yes," I say. "You spy on us all the time, don't you?" But I don't know how to say that everything feels different—and I don't know how or why.

"You . . . you have Boche and Mouschi, and I . . . I . . ." she begins, but she doesn't finish. Suddenly her head is in her hands and her hair is covering her face and she is sobbing words through her tears.

"I miss him! I miss him so much!" she says.

"Who?" I ask.

"Moortje," she says.

It's the name of her cat.

"Your cat?" I ask. She nods. At first I want to laugh. Then I try to imagine life without Mouschi. I can't.

I suppose Anne has Margot, but it's not the same. People have thoughts and opinions. They question you. Mouschi just is. I touch Anne's face. I put my arms around her and feel her break like water through my hands. Her body shakes but she still tries to be quiet . . .

"I . . . I . . . wish . . ."

"What do you wish?"

"That . . ." She sobs and hiccups. "That I had something of my own."

I don't say anything. Maybe I hold her a little bit tighter. I don't know. I let her speak, but all the time I'm thinking, *Does she mean me? Can it be me that might be hers alone?*

Slowly she calms down. She pushes her hair from her face. I help her. It's damp. Curly. She looks a mess. I've never seen a girl cry before. Not like that. Not like the whole world's ending. I don't know how long we've been up here, or what the others might be thinking. I don't know if she'll put it all in her diary. Is anything private for Anne? Some things should be kept just for yourself—shouldn't they?

"Sorry," she says, curtly. Abruptly. She's embarrassed.

"Don't be." So am I.

"Really, I'm just crying for everything we've lost."

"And doesn't writing and thinking about it just make it all worse?" I ask, but she only answers with another question.

"Do you miss things?" she says.

We're silent, again. She waits. I wait. Questions are dangerous, even if they're not going to be put in a diary and sent to the government.

"Of course!" I whisper.

"What things?" she says quietly. For a while I don't know what to say. Not because there aren't enough things, but because there are too many. So many things I miss. And if I let them all out, how will I ever get them all back in again? That's what I'm thinking in the darkness, as I feel her waiting for an answer.

"I miss the rain," I say after a while. "The rain on my face." And I can feel it as I say the words, rain falling fresh like pine needles on my face. I miss the rain with a physical ache, like a pain inside me.

"Outside!" breathes Anne. "I miss it more than I can say." She's still crying. I wish I could make it stop. I wish I could make everything all right. I wish I had words, like she has, that can explain things. But I don't. I don't tell her not to cry—that would be stupid. I hold her, although I don't know if I should. It feels odd. I don't know if I'm doing it right, or what she might say about it in her diary.

The tears go on until I forget everything except wanting to hold her tighter. I help her stand and we sit on the trunk and she puts her head on my shoulder, where I feel the tears slowly soak through my shirt. She is shaking.

I'm angry.

What chances do we have?

What choices?

None.

Outside the window the wind lifts the branches of the chestnut tree in the dark. A bird sings suddenly before remembering it's night, and Anne goes on crying. I never knew she was so sad. After a while I go and get her apron from where it's hanging to dry. She wipes her face.

"Better?" I ask, and then I blush. What a stupid thing to say. How can any of this be better? I wait for her to say so. She doesn't.

"Actually, yes," she says quietly.

"Oh, good," I say. "I'm glad."

She sniffs.

"Sometimes, I just . . . just get the feeling it's all too much, everything we've missed out on," she whispers. I nod.

"Mutti's chicken stock, with peas!"

"What?" she asks.

"Something else I miss," I say, and she smiles.

"Idiot! Can anything put the van Pelses off their food?"

"Could anything stop you writing your diary?"

"No," she laughs, and even though I knew that's what she'd say, it still hurts, knowing I come second to a notebook and pen!

I grab a huge pair of Pfeffer's pants off the line and offer them to her to blow her nose on. She giggles. "Put them back. I can't bear to even touch them."

"Anne?" I say, and she nods. "You do have something of your own."

She doesn't answer, just shakes her head.

"You do," I say. "You have your diary."

She looks up at me. Sudden. Sharp. And that's the way I'd draw her, if I could.

Just like that.

And that's the way I see her in my dreams. Am I awake or asleep? Alive or dead? I don't know. I only know that she's here with me all the time.

Her eyes are wide and her hands are busy writing, writing—recording each memory.

She hears everything.

Sees everything.

Just as she always has.

APRIL 9, 1944 — PETER AND ANNE TRY TO TALK ABOUT OUTSIDE

I'm almost asleep when Anne appears in the doorway with a cushion in her hands. We take it upstairs and make our own sofa. I put the cushion on a trunk and push it against two packing cases.

"There," I say.

"How much for the whole set?" she asks.

"It's not for sale, but to you it's free. Take a seat."

"Ah!" She sighs as she sits down. "There's nothing like a brandy and a cigarette after an evening spent listening to Mozart."

"I couldn't agree more!" I say. I'm learning how to play her games. I'm getting better. But so is she—at being quiet. We sit and stare out the window. The night takes longer to come now it's nearly summer. The sky's all shades of blue before turning black. The tree isn't just a silhouette of branches. It has fat, fat buds and curled leaves just waiting to burst. Buds that stand out against the dark. We sit down. Slowly I put my arm around her. Slowly she leans against me. Mouschi lies across our laps and keeps us warm. It is very cold. It's always cold. We wear so many clothes. "At least no one can see how thin we are," says Papi.

200

But we weren't thin, were we? Not really, not yet.

It's peaceful, for a while, being in the attic, with Anne.

"It's bad, isn't it?" she says.

I nod against her hair.

"Everything's running out," she says. "The food, the coal."
She stops for a moment.

"Even the Jews!" I whisper. We start to laugh. We know
we shouldn't. We know it isn't funny, and soon we stop. We
stop abruptly.

"Miep says that even the children steal."

"They're desperate!" I say.

"I know!" she says quickly. She knows how much I hate
it when she calls them slum children. We would do the same
if we were them, wouldn't we?

"I keep thinking of all those people in Hungary. How can
they kill so many, Peter? Do you think it's . . ."

"Shh," I say. Because there are no answers and there's
no point in the question. "We can't do anything—not yet."
She sits up and Mouschi curls away from her and onto
my lap.

"But we can," she says. "We can tell!"

"You can," I say.

"Anyone can," she says back.

"Maybe."

"Miep says it's terrible outside. The Dutch are turning on each other, stealing from each other."

"We're lucky," I say. "Lucky we're warm and fed and might last it out."

"I know. Well, reasonably warm," she whispers and snuggles in closer. "The thing about writing," she says suddenly, "is that it lasts forever."

I smile. "That's wonderful," I say, and I think that it must be. It must be wonderful to be Anne Frank and to never be alone because you always have something inside you. A story to tell. People to describe. Another idea to explore.

She leans against me, contented. These are the best moments. Not the moments where she longs for something I don't know if I can give her, but these moments. The easy moments, when I can tell her "Yes."

"Peter, I've been thinking, about what you said, about the things you want . . . and I—"

There's a low, urgent whistle and we leap up, guiltily, even though we've barely touched. Papi is on the stairs.

"Dr. Pfeffer says you've stolen his cushion." We grin at each other and rush downstairs.

"Oh, Anne!" Pfeffer grumbles, beating the cushion against his thighs. "I'll be jumping with fleas all night."

"No, no, it was only me who sat on it, and I don't have fleas." Anne smiles.

"Did you know fleas can jump several times their own height?" says Margot, and we all smile and try not to laugh at the thought of Pfeffer leaping anywhere at all.

"Good Lord," says Papi, "you could put us on your back, Pfeff, and leap us all the way to freedom."

"It's not funny!" Pfeffer says, and he storms off to his room.

I lie in my room and wonder what Anne was going to say next.

I was so busy thinking about Anne that I missed it. Because the footsteps were coming closer—and we weren't listening. Even when the break-in happened, we didn't really notice—we got too comfortable. We forgot how dangerous it was.

Outside.

We thought we would make it.

As soon as I step out from behind the bookcase I hear it. Two loud bangs, and my heart jumps. I wait for the sound of them again, but they don't come. I take off my shoes and run down the secret stairway. All the way down. Silently. The warehouse door is closed but a huge panel is broken off, the air's rushing through.

I run back up and ask Mr. Frank to help me with my homework. I can see Anne knows I'm lying, but I hope she won't say anything to Mutti. We pick up tools (well Father and I do, but Mr. Frank refuses again) and run down to the warehouse.

"Police!" shouts Papi and we hear footsteps running away down the street. In the dark we pick up the board and begin to replace it. It's impossible to do without making a noise. We try not to think of the centimeters between us and the outside, or about the sound of hammering so loud in the night.

"That'll do!" whispers Mr. Frank. We all take a deep breath and listen; unable to believe it's over. I breathe out, turn away. There's a loud, tearing noise and the board comes flying off the door. I turn back, a boot is sticking through the door, a big black boot, pushing itself into the warehouse, into the quiet and dark and safety. Threatening us. I swing my hammer at it and try to drive it straight back to the outside.

The hammer smashes against the splintered board. Father drives his ax against the floor in a fury. Sparks fly up. The footsteps run. Silence. Father and I lean against each other, breathing hard.

"Well, that seems to have done the trick," whispers Mr. Frank drily. "Let's put the board back up again."

We have only just lifted it when we hear more footsteps. We stop. Torchlight comes through the splintered door. Behind it are the shadows of a man and a woman.

"What the . . ." says Papi, and we all take off. Now we're the burglars. Papi and Mr. Frank rush to their wives. I run into the office and make a mess, as though there's been a burglary. I open windows. Papi remembers Dr. Pfeffer's in the toilet and helps him up the stairs. I close the bookcase carefully and stand behind it for a moment, listening. Nothing. I let the hammer hang in my hands, and wait.

There's no sound.

Mr. Frank gets the women upstairs. We open my window and listen. No sound.

And then we hear them. Footsteps in the office—on the staircase, and finally right at the bookcase.

The door rattles.

No one speaks.

No one moves.

I don't think any of us even breathes, but we all have the same thought. This is it. Now. But still none of us moves. Whoever is out there rattles the bookcase again. And again.

A tin falls off the shelves.

They know! I think. *Why else would they do this?*

We hear footsteps walking back through the office, closing windows and going down the stairs. But the light still shines beneath the door. Why have they left the light on? Will they come back to investigate? Have they gone to get tools? All these thoughts flash silently through my mind. We gather in the kitchen.

"All this excitement, I need the pot!" says Papi. And we realize the night buckets are in the attic and so we have nothing to piss in. In the end we use my bin—all of us. It reeks. It really does. It smells of all the piss and fear and shit in the room. Because that's what we are—afraid—scared for our lives.

I want to lie down with Anne under the table. I want to hold her in my arms. I want to have *something* to hold, *anything*—but all that's available is a cigarette. So I smoke. I don't inhale in case it makes me cough. I sit near the sink and wonder who they are, the couple with the torch. I hope they are a nice young Dutch couple out walking. I hope the fear in our faces made them pity us, not hate us.

I think my eyes close, but I don't think I sleep.

In the end I creep out to my room. Anne stands up as pale as a ghost in the dawn light, and follows me. We sit by my window and wait for the sun to come up. We don't say anything, but I think we're thinking the same thing. Is this it? Is this our last day? We sit very close together. So close I can feel her tremble. I have words in my mind. Words I can't say. Simple words.

Lie down and make love with me.

We are so cold. So tired. Lie down with me so we can sleep in each other's arms.

But we stay upright and silent at the window.

Like sentries.

Until, behind us, the others begin to whisper and wake. To make plans. And in the end I lie down on my bed alone. And fall asleep.

When I wake, Miep and her husband, Jan, are at the door.

I get up and stand in the kitchen doorway. Everyone's crying and talking. The place still smells terrible. I get the bleach and begin to tidy the smell away. The bin is full and leaking. I find a bucket. Mr. Frank helps me. It's heavy, but not as heavy as the feeling of fear inside me.

"Well done, Peter," he says, but the words slip off me. I nod anyway. It's hard to get all that fear to flush away down the toilet. We only have half an hour before the office staff arrive. We manage it in the end. When we come back, everyone has tidied the place as though nothing's happened. I stand and stare at the kitchen, at everybody talking. I remember the day I arrived. I feel the heat and remember how small and dark it felt. I feel dizzy with the lack of sleep. I imagine the rooms empty—everything gone, including us. *But we're already gone,* my mind whispers. There's no sign of us anywhere outside of these Annex walls.

Nothing for anyone except the office staff to miss if we're taken away.

I shake my head and try to focus.

Jan tells us the couple who saw us in the warehouse were Mr. van Hoeven and his wife, who deliver the potatoes. They didn't tell the police. They guessed someone was in hiding. Everyone starts talking and laughing with relief.

"But who broke in in the first place, and why?"

"How much longer can we hold on?"

We all sleep after lunch. I lie on my bed and stare at the cracks in the yellow ceiling. My eyes feel dry and gritty. Like there's salt in them. After a while I go down to the bathroom to wash them. Anne's there. She looks at me with her wide eyes.

"Do you still want to go to the attic?" I ask, and she nods. We go up. I put my arm around her shoulders and rest my head in her hair. I touch it with my fingers. She puts her arms around me. She does it shyly. She hugs me to her, or tries to. She's very small.

"Thank you," she whispers.

"What for?"

"Being so brave," she says.

"I'm not," I whisper.

"You fought for us," she says, "and then you cleared up the mess."

"We all did," I answer. The look of admiration in her eyes, and the feel of her arms around me are nice.

"Peter?"

"Yes?"

"I've been thinking, about what you said, and after last night I . . ."

Margot appears at the top of the steps.

"Come and sit down, Margot," I say, realizing how much we've left her out. "We're just sitting in the sun."

Margot smiles. "Ironic, isn't it?" she says. "Bad things happen and the sun shines. Tea's ready." And she disappears. We get up.

Downstairs everyone's happy with relief. They've made us real lemonade.

I wonder why we're celebrating.

I'm exhausted.

After a while I go to my room. I hope Anne might come. I hope the look of admiration might finally turn into a touch, a kiss, a . . . I fall asleep.

APRIL 14, 1944 — PETER IS IN LOVE
WITH ANNE

Anne talks and talks and talks. She doesn't even stop when my fingers run across her face, or touch her hair. I love the feel of her curls in my fingers. I love everything around me. I'm seeing it all differently since the break-in. I notice everything.

The world feels special and wonderful. A miracle: the sound of birds in the chestnut tree outside the window, the sun in a blue sky, the leaves. One day soon I'll come up here and the buds will be open. Wide open, and I won't have seen it happen.

I feel the sun on my face; watch it light up the skin on Anne's face. The light falls in a bar across her eyes as she reads me her poem about love and hope.

> *Work, love, courage and hope.*
> *Make me good and help me cope!*

"It's wonderful!" I say.

"Well," she smiles, "that's how you make me feel."

"Really?" I say. "I think that's how the *writing* makes you feel." And she stares at me. Gives me that sharp look.

"No," she says slowly. "Just sometimes, Peter, you know, the words come *after* the feeling."

Sometimes, in the camp, her words came to me. Appeared in my head out of nowhere. They came like a taunt. A curse. A dream from another world that has no meaning here.

They made me hope she died quickly. Quickly. That she walked into the chambers full of love, courage, and hope—and went out like a light. A bright light.

Not like this.

This living death.

I lie with my eyes wide open knowing that sleep won't come. That fear will instead. It happens sometimes, and there's nothing I can do to stop it.

I close my eyes tight. Squeeze them. I curl up into a ball and try to make myself small, hoping the fear will pass over me. But it's inside me. I can't escape it.

The house is hot. Airless. I can't open the window. There's something I need to remember.

I don't fall asleep; I just am asleep. Even in my dreams I'm naked and shivering and trying to remember something. In the dream everyone is naked. Everyone shivers. Everyone is Jewish, or broken or homosexual, or mad. We're all stumbling around, looking for a key. There are thousands of us— and yet somehow I'm alone.

I think I can hear the Westertoren bells again. I open my eyes—joyous, but it's not real, they're not here.

I don't fall asleep. I am asleep.

Anne's voice is calling me.

"Peter, Peter!" I feel her take my hand. I open my eyes, see her—and then I remember.

"I didn't unbolt the door!" I say, and sit bolt upright. She doesn't answer, just squeezes my hand.

"Come to breakfast," she says. My heart is beating so fast. I didn't unbolt the door. Every night I bolt the door so that no one can get in from the outside. Every morning I have to unbolt it, so that Mr. Kugler can use his key to get in. I can't speak. How did he get in? What's happened?

"Come on," says Anne, and she strokes my hand. "We should have reminded you," she says.

I get dressed. I can hear them in the kitchen, low voices muttering. When I go in they look at me. Not with anger, but with pity.

"Come, sit down, Peter," says Mr. Frank.

"Eat, darling," says Mutti. "Try and eat."

Papi just smiles at me. I try. I put the food on my plate. I can chew it but I can't swallow. Anne reaches across the table and touches my hand. Mr. Frank squeezes my shoulder.

"It's Peter I feel most sorry for in all this," says Mrs. Frank. I swallow. I try not to cry.

"What happened?" I ask. I have to know. They all look at Mr. Frank.

"Well," he says, "as you can imagine, Mr. Kugler couldn't open the door because it was bolted from the inside."

For a moment I think that's all he'll say. Everyone looks at him. Except Anne, who winks at me.

"He went to Keg's next door," he says.

Oh no, I think, *not Keg's.* They've already noticed things.

Now they must know that the door was bolted and so there must be someone inside. I swallow. No one says anything, but I hear them all breathe in. This is disastrous. It's bad. Very bad. No one has to tell me, or accuse me. I know it.

"He smashed the office window and got in that way." Silence. "Unfortunately the Keg's people noticed an open window in the attic. We've been careless. All of us," he says. I hang my head. Me most of all, I think.

"I'm so sorry," I say. Mutti smiles at me.

"It was me who opened the attic window," she says. "I wanted air-dried washing for once, and the day was so glorious."

"We should have reminded you, anyway," says Margot.

"Yes," says Anne, "it's your job to actually do it, but it's all of ours to remember."

"Yes," says Mr. Frank, "we're all responsible."

Dr. Pfeffer says nothing.

I stand up. "Thank you," I say. I go to my room. I want to be downstairs. I want to find Mouschi. I want to sit in the dark of the storeroom where no one can see me. But I can't face walking back through the kitchen to get there. I stand in the attic. The sun is shining. It's a beautiful day. The sky is blue. How could I forget? How could I put us all in so much danger? What's wrong with me?

Anne Frank's what's wrong with you.

"That's kind," I hear Mutti say, "but not now, Anne, later maybe. Leave him be for a while."

I sit in the sun on the floor. I don't know for how long. After a while I get up. I can't stay here forever. I can't change what has happened. If wishing worked, the war would be over. That's what Mutti says. So I get up. I go down the stairs. The Franks have gone, which is a relief.

Mutti hugs me. She doesn't need to say anything. I nod at Papi. "Bad luck, old chap," he says. "Could've happened to anyone."

But it didn't, I think. *It didn't happen to anyone. It happened to me.*

I go downstairs. To Mr. Frank.

"I put us in danger," I say. He doesn't disagree; he just nods—and then he smiles. "You made a mistake," he says, "but it's not you we're really in danger from, is it, Peter?"

"No," I say, "but . . ."

"What's done is done," he says quickly. "Don't dwell on it. Learn and move forward." I nod again.

"Could we do some French now?" I ask, because I want to be near him. I want to think about verbs and endings and all the things that create order and make sense.

"Of course," he says. He puts his book down. We practice spoken French. I'm not very good.

"*Bonjour!*" he starts.

"*Ça va?*" I say.

"*Ça va bien, merci. Et toi?*"

"*Ça va.*"

"*Qu'est que tu voudrais acheter ce matin?*" says Mr. Frank.

And the words come out of my mouth, in Dutch, not French. "Some freedom."

I blush. Mr. Frank smiles.

"Sadly, that's not something we can buy, Peter," he says. I don't say anything.

We start on irregular verbs.

———

Mr. Kugler's angry with us. We have to make changes: I have to patrol the building each night between eight-thirty and nine. We can't use the lavatory after nine-thirty. Pfeffer is complaining because he has to work in the bathroom, not the office.

But the worst thing of all is that I can't open my window at night. I understand why—the office next door have noticed it—but to lose my last bit of air from outside. It feels like a coffin lid banging shut.

Every time I think of what I've done, my stomach turns over and my heart beats fast. Anne says nothing, but whenever she can, she catches my eye and smiles at me.

At supper I can't eat—nobody mentions it, not even Pfeffer, which is kind. Everyone talks about something else. When she thinks no one's looking, Anne winks at me. At first I think it's a mistake, a twitch. But then just as her father is talking about the Allies and how they're certain to be here soon, she does it again. I look around. No one's noticed. She waits. And then she does it again. It makes me smile. I can't help myself. She blows me a kiss. After supper she sits on my bed with me.

"Hey! Move up a bit," she says, and then she tries to hold me. She reaches up to put her arms around me, but she's too small, so she gets a pillow and sits on it to make herself taller.

"Come here," she says, and she puts my head on her shoulder. She holds me so close that I don't feel alone anymore. She moves back and looks at me, questioning, but I can't speak. I hold her face in the palm of my hands and her name is all through me.

An-na, An-na, An-na.

Everywhere except on my lips.

I put her head on my shoulder. I can see my watch. I look at the minutes passing and know I must stand up soon because it will be eight-thirty, time to start my patrol. Life must start again. But I wish it didn't have to. Any of it.

I wish we could sit here, her head on my shoulder, my fingers in her hair. I stand up. So does she. I don't know what to say or how to thank her.

"I . . ." I begin, and she smiles, but I can't find the words. She puts her hand on my arm and turns to go.

"Anne?" I don't know whether I mean to kiss her mouth, her eyes, or her forehead. But I do mean to kiss her. I know that. She turns back and somehow I'm kissing her cheek, her hair, and the soft warmth of her ear. And then before I know it, she's gone.

I stand by the window. I take a breath. I touch my lips. A strand of hair's still caught between my fingers. "Anne?" I whisper her name. "Anne?" I shake my head and walk into the kitchen.

"All set?" asks Papi. I nod. "Good boy," he says.

But Mutti just stares at me. She doesn't say anything, not for a while, and then she touches my shoulder.

"Take care, Peter," she whispers, and I feel her eyes follow me out of the small room and all the way down the stairs.

I don't answer.

LATER THAT EVENING — PETER
EAVESDROPS ON HIS PARENTS

I stand by the door and listen. Papi is putting the bed down. Mutti is standing next to the sink, right by the door.

"Peter's not himself, Hermann, not himself at all—and we both know why, don't we? Did you see the look on that little minx's face as she came through his door! And it's not as though Edith Frank will do anything about it! Oh no! Her daughter's far too perfect to be the cause of anything. Well! What will she say when things have gone too far?"

"Ach!" says Father and I can hear him mutter.

"Do you know what that woman said to me? She said I was jealous, jealous of a fourteen-year-old girl—well, what do you think of that?"

Mutter, mutter is the only answer I can hear.

"Peter's only human. He's a boy, isn't he? And she's a girl," says Mutti.

More muttering from Papi.

"But how can you *know* he'll be sensible, Hermann? Would we have been?"

More muttering, then Mutti laughs as loud as she dares.

"If you think we would have waited in a situation like this, then you have no memory!"

There's a silence. I wait. The silence grows. The bed creaks. I move away from the door as fast as I can.

APRIL 16, 1944 — PETER'S IN THE WAREHOUSE

I'm never alone anymore. Even in the warehouse Anne's with me in my mind. I imagine us together in the secret dark and quiet. Think of how I might hold her as we breathe in the smell of spices—of what we might do together.

I walk past the table and feel something brush against my hip and fall. When I look down there's a pencil on the floor. I think nothing of it. I simply pick it up and balance it back on the table, wondering how it got there.

There were clues. Plenty of them. Someone was watching.

The time is coming closer. But I'm not listening, not watching.

I'm too full of longing . . .

For Anne.

We spend all our spare time in the attic. Holding each other. Talking and talking and talking. I never knew I had so many words in me. So many thoughts. Anne is amazing.

"What is love anyway?" she says one day. "I mean, do you have to be married to feel it?"

"No," I say.

"Exactly! Look at our parents, are they shining examples of how to love each other?"

"Well," I say, hesitant, "I do think mine love each other, even if they argue." I think of Papi remembering Mutti in pink silk. I think of their bed creaking. I don't say anything, just in case she puts it into the diary.

"Well, Daddy doesn't love my mother."

"Don't you think so?" I ask. "But they never argue."

"Exactly! No passion!"

I think about that. I wonder why Anne and I never argue.

I'm lying on my bed with my arms around her. It feels as natural as Mouschi lying in my lap. Sometimes I slip my hand beneath the fabric of her dress and feel the curve of her shoulder.

Mouschi is always pushing and squeezing in between us. Jealous. I push him away.

I think Anne is crying again; silently beneath my shoulder. The tears are soaking into my overalls. How do so many feelings fit in someone so small? I hold her a little tighter. Say nothing. Does she know I can tell? Does she think I'm lying here with her in my arms imagining she's smiling? Why doesn't she say anything? Why does she never talk of her sadness? At eight-thirty we stand up. It's time to go. She stands by the window. It makes me smile, the way she always does the same thing. She stands by the window to say goodbye. She's shaking. I reach out. I think if I hold her I can stop her shaking. Not forever, but at least for now. I hold out my arms. She throws her arms around me and I'm pushed back against the wall. I feel the warm weight of her on my neck. The soft press of her lips on my cheek. It's too sudden, it takes me by surprise. And then my mouth finds hers.

And once it's there I can't stop.

It doesn't matter what I think, or how I try so hard to respect her father—to be a man and refuse to take what isn't mine.

Her body is against mine, clinging to me. Our mouths press. And I can't stop. I don't want to stop. Until Anne pulls away. We stare at each other. Her eyes still gleam with tears and something else. Something I don't know or recognize.

"Anne." But she doesn't stay. She doesn't give me time to say anything more. She turns and goes. And a thought comes.

She can't wait to get that in her diary.

Mouschi stalks around my ankles, his tail high and angry. I pick him up.

"What?" I say, sitting down. He holds his head up, pushes it into my hands, waiting for the feel of my fingers behind his ears. And then he flattens himself out along my lap. What if it were Anne? What if it were her lying across my lap with my hands running down her body?

"No," I whisper to myself, but what I really mean is yes.

We're scared.

Scared that this is our only chance.

Not tomorrow.

But here.

And now.

I can't wait to be alone with her again. I rinse my mouth out and wash my face. I'm sitting ready at my desk when she comes in.

"Peter?" she asks as soon as she sits down. "*Do* you think I should talk to my father about us?"

"Of course," I say quickly, "you must do what you think is right." But my heart sinks. Is she telling him so she'll have a good excuse for stopping us? She nods at me, distant, formal, like she was my secretary, like that kiss never happened. Has her body forgotten? Mine hasn't. Last night as I fell asleep I felt the push of her small breasts against my chest. Sharp and sudden, like lust. I realize she's still talking.

"You are worth my trust, aren't you, Peter?" I blush. Don't say anything. What does she mean? What does she want? *You started it,* I feel like saying, *and now I can't stop. Can't stop wanting you.*

Anne talks and talks until dusk.

I'm silent.

"Are you all right?" she asks. I don't say anything for a while.

"I could watch you forever," I say in the end. "Listen to you forever."

"Wait a minute," she says.

When she comes back she has something in her hands. It's her diary. I stare at it. Anne's precious thing, so precious her father keeps it in a briefcase by his bed at night. (As though it wasn't hard enough already, hiding the eight of us, he has to hide her diary too!) She holds it out to me. I take it in my hands. I stare at it.

"Go on," she says. "I've marked the page. I've been thinking about it ever since the break-in, and trying to say it, Peter, but somehow it's always easier to write."

I open where it's marked. Her handwriting's neat and small. I read it quickly. The words jump out at me. She's asking about love, about what it might mean. She's saying it's physical, as well as everything else; some of the words leap at me. She's saying love can't be shared, that it's only ever between two people. I blush when I read that. I think about my Liese, and her Peter. I wonder if that's what she means.

I read the words twice over. I look up at her; she's watching me, waiting. I try to really think about what she's saying but all I can actually do is wonder if she means it. "Does virtue really matter?" she asks. "Do you have to be married, or is it acceptable to love another person, physically, as long as it is only them?"

"Do you really mean all that?" I ask. She nods at me. "I've thought about it a lot. I know it could all end tomorrow."

"Even the bit about losing your virtue?"

"If the person's worth it, and isn't in love with anyone else." She stares at me hard, with her all-seeing eyes. "That's what I really mean by can I trust you," she says. "I couldn't bear to be second to anyone." She laughs again.

"Really?" I ask. "Anne Frank," I say, "you're utterly unbelievable!"

"Thank you!" She smiles and pretends to curtsy.

I close the diary and hold it in my hands. I stare at her standing by the window. Anne Frank, small, determined, and thinking—always thinking. Always hoping. Always curious. Never able to be second to anyone, although we're all second to her writing.

This moment. I am full of it. Full of her. There is no Liese, just me—and Anne.

"Yes!" I say. "You can trust me. I'll never put you second!"

I hand the diary back.

"When we get out of here, you'll forget me, won't you?" she says suddenly. She tips her head sideways. Gives me her film-star smile—and now she's the other Anne Frank, a girl of a million disguises, and I never know which one is real. I'm furious. How can she treat me like this, playing games as though putting her over Liese was nothing at all?

"That's not true, Anne, you can't think that about me!"

Because I'll never forget Anne Frank—whatever happens.

"Why not?" she asks. She raises her eyebrows, pouts her mouth. I turn away. I want to smack her, hard. I want to wake her up. This is not a game. You're not a film star, Anne, and I'm just a boy with an ache in his groin! Shall we talk about that?

"I think you'd better go."

She picks up her diary and begins to leave.

"Peter?" she asks, her small face white now. "I . . ."

"Sorry, Anne, I'm sorry, but you change so quickly, and you play games, and sometimes it's just . . ."

"I know," she says. "But, Peter, I'm confused too."

"Are you?"

"Of course I am."

"It doesn't feel that way!"

She shakes her head at me—at herself.

"I know," she says again, "it's awful. Sometimes I think I'm only really me in my diary!"

"Sometimes I hate your diary!"

"Why?"

"Because it's always first and I'm always second, and sometimes it feels like you only spend any time with me so you've got something to put in it."

"Peter!"

"Well it does!"

She sits down again. We both take a deep breath.

"I . . . I . . . wouldn't write about it if you didn't want me to," she says after a while.

"Really?"

She blushes. "Well maybe I'd put some of it in a story, but that's not the same. Is it?"

She stares at me.

"Isn't it?" I ask. "How would you know, Anne? Has anyone ever put you in a story? Do you know how it feels to be Hans in your 'Cady's Life'?"

She blushes and clutches her diary to her chest.

"You noticed?"

"It was hard to miss."

"Well," she says defiantly, "it's not deliberate. I don't think about it, I just write and then . . . well . . . it's there."

"Yes, it's on a page where it looks like the truth—even if it isn't."

"Is that how it feels?" she asks.

"It feels like being stolen." The words are out before I know it. She stares at me.

"Sorry." She swallows, her eyes blinking with tears. "I'm sorry. I didn't know, but I can't stop. I mean writing's like . . ."

"Being in love with someone else?"

Again the words just come, but as soon as they're there I

know it's true. Just as I love Liese, Anne loves writing. Both of us have someone else.

Anne doesn't answer, she just runs from the room.

———

I go all the way down to the warehouse. I sit with my back to the wall. I raise my head and stretch my neck. I take a deep breath and let my head fall forward.

Is it right for me to long for us to make love if it's only because we might die?

What if Liese survives?

What if I let Mr. Frank down?

What if Anne doesn't mean any of it?

I wait for Boche to appear, but he doesn't come.

Where are you, Boche? I don't know what I'll do if he doesn't come back. I can't imagine not having him here: the smell of the air in his fur, the touch of his paws as he walks up my body. Where are you, Boche?

"I don't know. I don't know," I whisper to myself.

I don't know anything.

I don't even know what's right or wrong anymore.

APRIL 30, 1944 — MR. FRANK
QUESTIONS PETER

"Peter?" Mr. Frank is standing at the door. I stand up.

"I thought I could trust you," he says.

"You can, sir."

"I don't think you understand, Peter," he says gently. "This isn't just about house politics, this is about my daughter."

I nod.

"Are you in love with her?" he asks.

I shrug. "I don't know," I say. "We enjoy each other's company. I think . . . we make each other happy, maybe."

"And desire?" he says. "I was a boy once too, Peter."

Not like this you weren't, I think. But again I say nothing. Have I let him down?

"I can control myself," I say after a while.

He takes a deep breath. "You might and Anne might, but together it can be a different story," he says.

Is that how you ended up married to Mrs. Frank? I put my head down quickly, hoping the thought doesn't show. But when I look up he's smiling. "You can't control love, Peter! The best you can do is stay out of its way. That's what I'm asking; that you don't put yourself in its path. That means not spending hours alone together. Do you understand?" I nod again, but I don't speak.

After a while he stands and leaves.

So she did decide to tell her father about us.

Why?

I go down to the warehouse, but I can't find Boche anywhere. I'm worried; would anyone eat a cat? The thought circles around my mind. I sit in the dark and wait. And wait. But Boche is gone, and however much I want to, I can't go and find him.

MAY 5, 1944 — ANNE IS FURIOUS

"We can do what we want!" Anne says. "They don't know what it's like to be us. To have missed out on so much! We have to trust our own judgment and do what *we* think is right, don't we, Peter?"

"As long as it's just between us," I say. She glances away; she can't meet my eyes. I wait, and when she does look back at me, suddenly, somehow, we're alone together with that silent question in our eyes, searching each other for an answer.

The air shivers under the eaves. Anne trembles in the heat. She blows a wisp of hair away from her face.

"It's so hot," she whispers. She lies down in the patch of sunlight and stretches, soaking up the heat. She closes her eyes. Slowly I stand up and move a sack of beans onto the trap door. The air's so still, I can hear our breathing. I lie down next to Anne, lean on my elbow and stare at her in the sunlight. She has the slightest smile on her face, but she doesn't open her eyes.

"Stop staring!" she says.

"You're beautiful," I say, and it's true. She is.

I lie flat and reach for her hand; our fingers curl within each other's. I turn my head and kiss her forehead. She raises her head, touches my lips with hers. She opens her eyes. We stare at each other as we kiss.

"Anne?" I whisper. She nods her head, eyes wide.

My heart lurches. I don't know what's happening. I try and smile but I can't. My face won't move.

I lift my hand and reach beneath her hair. Her neck is so small I can almost fit one hand around it. I'm shaking. I touch the bone where her head joins her neck, small and delicate.

Anne shivers slightly. Our eyes are locked. I run my fingers all the way down her spine and feel her breathing change, like Mouschi's, almost to a purr. She stretches and sighs, turns on her back, closes her eyes. I rest my hand on her stomach. And concentrate. On keeping it there.

"Anne?"

"Peter?"

Her eyes open. Our faces move closer. I put my hands in her hair. It's soft and wiry all at the same time. We move closer and closer until we're pressed up tight against each other in the sunlight, her skin warm beneath my fingers. She's like the curve of a perfect piece of wood beneath my hands, only soft and real and here and now. I hold her so close I forget where she begins and I end.

She moves back swiftly. Sharply. And gasps. "Oh!" And looks down at me. I sit up.

"It's all right," I whisper quickly, moving back. But it's not all right. Everything's returning: the sunlight, the window, the hanging washing. It's all spinning toward me as Anne moves away. I hold on to her hand.

"Peter!" she whispers. "Peter!"

I take a breath, try to make sense of everything, remember who I am, where I am. "Anne?" I ask.

"I'm fine," she says. "I just, it's just . . . well, it's so much more *real,* than I thought!"

I nod. She grips my hand.

We sit together, silent, until my breath returns, until the words come back with the world that for just a moment had dissolved completely into sunlight, and Anne.

"Anne."

"Mmm."

"Don't put this in your diary."

"I won't." She lets got of my hand. "Peter?"

"Mmm."

"You know, I'm not just with you for something to put in my diary."

"Thanks," I say. I stand up and look out the window. Outside the sky's a pale blue, and the sea a strip of dark in the distance against it. I look at it waiting for my body to stop aching with longing, to settle.

We're silent for a while.

"Will you stay here, in Holland, when the war ends?" Anne asks.

I sigh. We lean against opposite ends of the window.

"No. I think I'll go somewhere warm."

"Don't you want to be Dutch?"

"I don't want to be anything," I say.

"How can you say that?"

"Why *can't* I say that?"

"It's not fair," she says passionately, and I wish she felt like that when she's in my arms, the way she sounds now. But she doesn't. "If we were Christians we'd just be people! If we do anything wrong it's like the whole Jewish race has done it! Why is that?" she mutters.

"Of course it's like that, Anne, but maybe some of us make it like that, by thinking we're so special."

"We have to, we have to preserve our tradition, we're under attack. We should be proud!"

"We are proud. Maybe *too* proud!"

"Peter!"

"I like the idea of being responsible for *my* actions, not the whole race's. Is that so wrong?"

"No, but . . ." And then she begins to giggle. When Anne giggles . . . Well, the sound of it is like a light in a dark room. Really. Or that feeling you get when the pencil does the drawing for you. Soon she's rolling on the floor.

"What? What is it?"

"Imagine," she gasps, "if you were the only boy left . . ."

"That's not funny."

"Peter van Pels, last man standing, it is your job to procreate the race!"

And now we're both on the floor, laughing, holding on to each other, trying to be quiet.

"You . . . you'll be like my old algebra book." She laughs. "All used up. So many names in you!" I'm now laughing. And then I imagine the lines of girls, waiting. Good Jewish girls, doing their duty, hoping to perpetuate the race. Anne is still lying on the floor, shoulders shaking.

"Anne!" No answer.

"Anne, it's not funny!" She stops. She stops as suddenly as she started.

"I know," she says.

We're silent. We sit apart with the whole world and all its hatred lying in the air between us.

"Sorry," she whispers.

"Me too," I answer.

"So where would you go?" she asks after a while.

"Far away," I say. "Somewhere where the sun shines. You know the word I love?"

"No."

"El Dorado!"

She laughs. "Why?"

"I don't know. It means gold, doesn't it? The thing you want, that you'll discover. The thing that will make you rich!" and as I say the words I realize I mean *her*. Anne. She's the thing I want to discover.

"Oh," is all she says. "Not all riches are about money!"

———

Later, when we meet on the stairs, I call her my El Dorado so she'll know that I didn't mean money!

"Sweet boy," she says, "you can't call a person that."

But you can. You can if you know that they are better than gold and are yet to be discovered.

Was there ever really a world like that, where we spoke and laughed and thought aloud?

Where we weren't stripped bare and made to know what a man is when there is nothing left of him but thought for his own survival.

Mr. Frank saved me from that.

At least, while we were together.

Did I tell you about the soup? Did I tell you how I longed to fill my stomach? That if I could get a few extra pints warm inside me, I'd take it. Forgetting how it will press against my bladder in the night, and wake me.

Once I got up to piss and it was freezing. The stars were so high. So far away. So clear. So cold. But for some reason, that night, I could see how beautiful they were. And I stood there. Staring. And for a moment. Just a moment. I felt human again. And then the moment passed.

MAY 26, 1944 — PETER WANTS ANNE, ANNE WANTS TO WRITE

Everything's changing. The invasion is coming closer. The whole Annex is upside down. One minute the bombardment will come tomorrow. The next we'll never escape because the Nazis will drown us like rats, will flood the whole of Holland if they can't have it to themselves.

Outside people are starving. We are too. I would love the taste of something fresh in my mouth, something that hasn't spent months in a barrel. Everything is rotten.

Everyone is hoping we'll be free by the end of the year. Anne is so excited by the thought of outside, by the idea that her diary will be a testament to what happens in hiding.

"But it's so boring in here most of the time!" I say.

"It depends how you put it," she answers, which is a bit worrying.

I escape to the storeroom, but someone's knocked over a bag of flour. In my heart I hope it's Boche, even though I know he'd never be so clumsy. I don't know whether to leave it or clean it up.

"Have you walked in it?" asks Mr. Frank.

"No."

"Then leave it." He looks worried. That means I can't go down there all weekend. I feel even more trapped. I go down to the warehouse instead.

The door's stuck, but finally I get it open. Mouschi follows me in. He crouches down, his back arched and nose to the ground, his eyes staring up at nothing. He does the same thing with sunlight sometimes in the attic. He watches and watches and then he pounces on the light and nothing's there! But this is different, unnerving, like he's watching an invisible enemy. Suddenly I wonder if he can see an invisible Boche, playing in the air. I shake my head.

Slowly I slide back up the wall and slip toward the door. That's when I see the wedge pushed back—and realize that's what made the door stick. I know right away that there's nothing I can do. Nothing. I can't put it back. I can't close the door and put the wedge in on the right side. I stare at it. I stare at it as though I could make it go away. Who put it there?

I go through the door and close it. I tell Mr. Frank.

"Thank you, Peter. Let's just keep this to ourselves, shall we?" I nod. I don't go back downstairs.

I don't want to anymore. I make sure Mouschi stays upstairs. There's still no sign of Boche. I know in my heart he's gone. I've known it for weeks, but I keep on hoping, keep on thinking he might stalk in when I least expect it, and put his head beneath my palms.

Anne is lit up. Sometimes when I touch her, I'm amazed she's not burning with heat, with passion for all the words and ideas and hope that come pouring out of her.

But it's not passion for me.

"Peter?"

"Mmm?"

"I'm writing! I'm writing!"

"I know!"

"I want people to know, Peter. I want them to feel what we feel. What it's like to be scared. What it's like to look out the window and see your own people led away while you're safe in your bed. What it's like to eat while they starve. If they know, if they feel it too, then they can never do this again, can they?" Her eyes are alight. Blazing. Burning. They are amazing.

"But we're *not* safe in our beds, Anne, are we?" I say gently. I don't know why I have to say it. Anne knows it already. Anne fears it more than any of us. Quite often she shakes with fear. I can feel it inside her when I hold her. That she is always trembling. With fear. With excitement. With despair. And now, with hope. It's her diary. That's what does it. It means she remembers instead of forgets. It means she hopes instead of just waiting, like the rest of us.

"But we've lasted so long. Waited so long, Peter! Don't you think . . . ?" And then she stops herself.

"What?" I ask. She slows herself down. I watch her do it. She wants to shout her words from the rooftops, but she is trying to slow herself down, to hold on to herself. But really, she's flying. Flying above us all. Flying high in the air on words and ideas and writing, writing, writing.

"Don't you think God is saving us for a reason?" she says. "A purpose? Anyway, despair is a sin, especially when we have all this!" And she throws her arms out toward the window, where the sun is shining through the leaves of the chestnut tree, full of summer. And Anne is like that too—full of hope and life and belief. It's exhausting.

"Why should he?" I say.

"What?" She looks away from the window, toward me. She looks shocked, surprised that I need to say anything at all. After all, she's said it all already, hasn't she?

I swallow. I say the words. "Why should God save us, Anne, when he hasn't saved so many?"

She stops. She doesn't answer for a while.

"I dreamed of Hanneli, my friend, the other day. Did you know her? She was taken away." She doesn't have to say any more. We all have our dreams of those who are gone. We don't speak of them. We don't have to. They're written on our faces the next day, in our dull eyes, our slow movements. We all notice. We all move around that person carefully. Maybe we're being kind. Maybe we're scared of being infected. I don't know. All I know is that we give each other time. And space. And that we don't talk about it.

"We all dream, Anne," I say. I think of Liese's shaven head, heavy in my hands. I bite my lip. I don't want Anne's dreams. I have enough of my own.

"I was cruel to Hanneli, Peter. If I ever get out of here, I'll make it up to her. I will." She's frantic now. Panicking. I sigh. Everything Anne feels she feels more than anyone else.

"You were a child, Anne, like your father said, children are often cruel without meaning it, like animals."

"But what if she's dead? What if I never get the chance to say sorry?" she wails. She looks so tiny. So lost. So frail. So I hold her. I can't help it. I know I shouldn't. I know in the end it won't make anything better—and that I can never make her love me more than she loves ideas and books and writing—but it soothes her. And she's warm. And for a while I feel strong. And sure. Sure that for once I'm doing something good. Holding things safe in my hands. No. Holding *her* safe in my hands.

———

I dreamed of her last night.

I was high on a trapeze. I was upside down. Swinging.

246

And then the people came. Their bodies fell down around me like rain. I held out my hands to catch them. A touch. A clasp. But they all fell through my fingers in the end. Down and down into the distance. Thousands of them. All with shaven heads and accusing eyes. I held my palms out, reached and felt fingers. Held tight. And then I heard her voice: "Peter," she said, and our eyes met.

"Anne?" Her eyes held mine. Her eyes were trying to tell me something, but I couldn't hear it. And she began to slip. Slip through my fingers . . .

Until she fell. Until she was one of a hundred, thousand, million bodies like raindrops—falling. And then it stopped. And the world was empty. I swung upside down in the darkness. With nothing but the torn piece of paper she'd left me, fluttering in my hands.

The next morning everyone steps around me. Gives me space. And I know the dream is written on me.

You see? We knew. We knew it was coming. That the net was closing. That we were just fish, really, already flapping and struggling for air. We used to joke about it, in the old days, back in Zuider Amstellaan. "What will they ration next?" Papi would say. "The air we breathe?"

Yes, Father, yes. They turned the air into gas and killed you with it.

Is this just another dream?

Another nightmare?

Another telling?

And in the end, the thing that always happens will happen again.

You'll smile and stand up. Make some comment that proves you haven't heard me at all.

And then you'll walk away.

Isn't that how it goes?

JUNE 6, 1944 — THE INVASION HAS BEGUN

The British are bombing all along the northern French coast.
I look out the window. The rain's falling on the canal. I wish
I could feel it on my face. I wish it like I've never wished for
anything before. If I could have any power in the world, I'd be
invisible. I'd go outside and still be safe. I say so. Anne glances
up at me.

"Don't be silly," she says, and flicks another page of her
magazine. "If you were invisible you wouldn't really exist."

I think about that as I watch her turning the pages, staring, smiling. After a while she looks up.

"Well? It's true, isn't it?"

I think it's true that Anne has had enough of me.

"I'm not sure. I mean, I'd still be here really, wouldn't I?
And . . . and I could go outside."

She sighs, exasperated. I do that to her these days. Make
her sigh. Mr. Frank was upset and angry with her for seeing
me, and now she's upset and angry with me for still wanting
her, when all she wants is the day of liberation to come and
to work on her diary.

"Would you though, Peter?" she says. "Would you really
be you if you could go out there? Would you be the same

person with the same set of experiences? Honestly?" She's smiling now, laughing. She's playing with me. All of my thoughts feel meaningless when she's like this. I turn away. I don't know. I don't know. I don't know anything, do I?

I stare at the window. I'd like to hit it. I'd like to put my fist through it and feel it shatter. I'd like to see blood. But it feels like if I tried, the glass would only bend and trap me. Like Anne's mind does. She gives a big, loud sigh.

"Nothing to say?" she asks. "Well there's a surprise." And she turns back to her magazine in disgust. I wait. I wait until the anger isn't so loud in me.

"I've got lots to say."

She looks up. "What then?"

The silence in the attic stretches. I'm going to say it. I can feel the words rising up in me, about to be spoken.

And so can Anne. She holds her hand out suddenly, as though she could stop me. "Peter . . . I . . ."

It's late. The attic's bathed in late spring twilight. Dusk. That's good. That makes the words come more easily.

"I'm Peter," I say. And my own name echoes inside me. I hear Liese's voice calling me in my dreams. I hear Anne say my name as she slips through my fingers.

"Peter van Pels," I say, and for some reason my name sounds wonderful to me. "Peter van Pels." I say it again. I am

Peter. I am here, and it feels like a miracle to me. Not just that I'm alive, but that anyone is, ever.

"Well, that's your name, that's true, but it's hardly an identity, is it?" says Anne.

I laugh. It sounds odd.

"It's enough for me," I say. "That's all I want to be. Peter van Pels. Not Jewish, not Dutch, not German, just me!"

It's a strange feeling hearing my thoughts out loud.

Anne's voice is a hiss in the dark.

"Yes, Peter van Pels, too cowardly to own up to being a Jew! Too cowardly to want to tell our story!"

"No!" Because that's not what I mean. I'm not a coward because I didn't stand in the street and fight to the death for Liese, although I wish I had, and I'm not a coward because I wish I could be invisible enough to go outside. I'm a coward because I can't speak. Like right now, in the dark with Anne's voice accusing me. The words have gone. I'm a coward because I don't know how to be me. That's what I want to say.

"You're wrong!" is all that comes out of me. Her fury is like a fist in the dark.

"One day," she cries, "everyone will know what they did. Our story, not theirs. And we'll be proud to be Jews!"

"Good!" I say. And I mean it. "I wish we could all be whatever we wanted, that's all that matters. That we're all human! We can be anything, Anne, as long as it isn't a Nazi. That's all."

She isn't listening. "We have to survive, Peter. We have to give witness!"

I sigh.

"That's your way, Anne," I say quietly.

"What other way is there?" she asks. "Are you really happy pretending none of this is happening, to spend all our time kissing on the floor?"

"What?"

She blushes.

"Is that how you see it?" I ask.

"I asked *you* the question: what other way is there left, except to tell our story?"

I don't know the answer to her question. I just know it's not the *only* question. Listening to her makes me feel like the weight of survival's suffocating me. But Anne won't let me lie down. She won't let me sleep. She's like a tram bell going off in my ear. I sit down next to her.

"Anne," I say, "what if we lived in Holland, but it was just a name?"

"Well it is a name." She shakes her head, irritated.

"I know, but . . ." She laughs at me before I can finish. I go on anyway. "But what if Holland or Amsterdam were just places? I mean, imagine if you only said those words because

252

they were somewhere you wanted to go." I'm not explaining very well. I can feel it.

"Well, that's obvious," she says. She laughs. I feel like a clown getting the jokes wrong.

"Is it?" I ask, wondering. Has she really understood so easily what has taken me so long?

"Of course," she says.

I nod. "So Holland is just Holland to you? Not Holland the place that saved us; or Amsterdam that is now so dangerous because people are starving and might betray us?"

"Oh," she says, and she ruffles my hair. "You mean people attach meaning to places. Yes, *of course* I understand that, Peter!" She's so quick it tires me.

"Well what if we didn't?"

Her hand falls away from my hair. "What do you mean?"

"What if we didn't attach meaning to places, or religions?" I admit I whisper the last bit.

"That's not possible, you sweet-hearted twit. It's not human," she says.

"Isn't it?" The words come out too loud. "If there was no Germany, or Holland, or France, or Belgium, there'd be no one to fight, would there?"

For once she's silent. It gives me courage. "And Anne, if there were no Christians or Jews—if we were allowed to be just people, just Peter and Anne . . . No! I mean that *is* what we are. We're not just Jews. We're us, here in the attic, feeling what we feel." I gulp. "Like me wanting you—and you wanting to save the world. I mean does one of us always have to be the right one? Can't *both* things be true?"

I'm shaking. I've never said so much, or meant it so much. I reach out for her hand but she pushes me away. She stands up, a shadow in the faint light from the window. She doesn't say anything for a while. Neither do I. For a moment I hope that she might turn and take me in her arms, that she might be the Anne who knows this might be our only chance, and wants to take it.

"I'm grateful to you, Peter," she says.

"Why?"

"Because you showed me something."

"What?"

"That it's my writing I want, really."

"Oh."

"And that everything else, even Father and you, have to come second."

"I know, but I still thought we might be . . ."

"I can't, Peter. I can't think about anything else. Except that it's ending and that we have the chance to tell. Nothing else matters, not to me, and I can't believe you don't want to be a Jew anymore."

"No! I was born Jewish, I can't deny that. I don't even want to, but it's up to me what I do about it. And I'd never not support Jews, or anyone else being treated like we are."

"Do you believe in anything?" she asks.

"Yes!" I say. And the word feels good. Even if it means that she walks away, even if it makes no difference to anyone else, because it matters to me. It's what I think.

"Like what?" she sneers at me. I turn away from the look on her face so I can put the thoughts into words.

"I believe in people."

"Right," she says, "and not God?" I can hear her shock. I'm shocked myself. Shocked at finally hearing the things I've been thinking said out loud. They sound final. They sound real. They sound like a door shutting between us. A door that we'd only just opened.

"I don't know," I say. "It's not the idea of God I don't like, it's the choosing. It's that one religion is meant to be better than the other. I mean, how is God deciding any different from Nazis deciding, I don't see . . . ?"

She gasps as though I've hit her, knocked the breath out of her.

"No, you don't see," she says, "but I do! You don't believe in anything at all!"

"I believe in *people,* Anne! In you and me and even Dr.

Pfeffer. In all of us." I want to say more, like if I have to die, then I don't want to die for being a Jew, I want to die for . . . for being me . . . for hating Nazis and everything they stand for. I don't want them to choose *why* I die . . . I want to re-sist . . . But the words have stopped. We don't say any more for a long, long time. Anne waits at the window. I want to put my arm around her, but I can't. I want to hold her, but I can't.

She's somewhere else now.

Beyond me.

"You're a coward, Peter," she says at last, "because you're afraid of being a Jew who'll stand up and be counted."

I can't answer her. Maybe she's right. Maybe it's true. I don't know. I only know this. "I'm not a practicing Jew and we both know that makes no difference, Anne, that they'll still kill me if they find us."

"It can't be a *choice,*" she hisses. "Maybe later, but not now, Peter! Not in the middle of all this!"

I wish, more than anything else in the world, that I could fall into her arms and say, "I'm sorry, I know what you mean, none of it matters, let's just hold each other." But I can't. I have to be me, to understand who I am. If Anne's taught me anything, it's this. It doesn't matter what we *want,* what mat-ters is who we *are,* and we can't change that, not even if we were the last people left on earth. I sigh. "But that's what I *am* saying, Anne," I say quietly, "that for me it *is* a choice."

"You're wrong," she says. "You're deserting us."

"Anne! I would never leave you!" The pain of her words twist inside me and I can't help it, I reach out for her.

"You're already gone!" she says as she leaps away from me. My hand falls through the air and she turns quickly and runs down the stairs.

I sit in the attic.

"Great!" I whisper to myself. "Well done, Peter!"

I want her to come back. I want to hold her. I want to make love to a girl. I want so many things, but what I *need* is to know who I am. Because if I don't know that, I can only ever be what they say I am.

A Jew.

In Auschwitz there is only one way to count a Jew.

Stand us in the freezing cold or rain or heat in groups of five.

And add us up.

Do I count?

No. I am just a number, a body. A cog in the wheel that must be counted.

JUNE 7, 1944 — PETER FEELS HOPE

The sun has gone. The wind and rain howl around the house all night. I can't sleep. The wind whistles down the pipe by the head of my bed.

Outside, terrible things are happening: everything is running out. There is no food. There is no money. People are starving. We are too. How will we survive? Will we survive? We don't know.

Outside, wonderful things are happening too: the invasion has begun and Churchill has said the end is in sight. We are frightened to hope. Mutti and Papi say, "Ach! It's just a trial, not the real thing," but excitement lingers beneath our words like the stink of Mouschi's pee in the attic. You can't see it but you can smell it.

It's the smell of hope.

JUNE 11, 1944 — THE DAY BEFORE
ANNE'S BIRTHDAY

I want to buy Anne something beautiful for her birthday. I want her to know that we can still be friends, can't we, even if we're different?

And now we have to find a way back to friendship. The memory of touching her, wanting her, already feels strange somehow—like a violation. Sometimes you don't know until you try.

It was wrong.

It was right.

It was all we had.

I ask Miep if she'll buy Anne some flowers. She gives us such hope, Miep. Caen has fallen to the British. Hope is in the air. The Annex is alive with it.

In the end I ask her to buy some peonies. Pink and young and not yet quite opened—but they will be so full and beautiful when they do. She gives me a strange look when I describe it like that—and then she smiles and nods. The bunch she brings is perfect. I put it on my desk and stare at the flowers all evening. I draw them. But I can't get it. I can get a likeness, but not their essence; not the fresh, alive, unopened green smell of them. I see them in my sleep. Shining in the dark. And when I open my eyes they're still there. I can't wait to give them to her.

She was about to be fifteen. She was clever and con-temptuous and funny and thin and sometimes, when she smiled, she was beautiful. As beautiful as the world outside seemed. I don't know if she'll ever be sixteen.

Anne looks at them. My flowers.

"Thank you, Peter, they're lovely."

I don't say anything. Once I would have wanted to explain. I would have felt sad. I would have wanted them to be perfect for her, but now, well, if Anne doesn't like them, there's nothing I can do.

"I enjoyed looking at them, all evening," I say, and she glances at me and away again. She's unhappy. I know how that feels. To have a birthday in the Annex, an anniversary. A time of thinking about what's past, and worse, what might be about to come. Birthdays aren't joyous for us, despite the news of the invasion.

And the weather is terrible. Really.

Anne fiddles with the little gold bracelet on her wrist that Margot gave her. They giggle together, and play "Remember."

"Remember when we used to sit on the roof at Merwedeplein?" "Remember at the Jewish Lyceum when that couple came to get married?"

We're all remembering the past, the way you only can when you're hopeful about the future.

Mr. Frank looks at me, and smiles. I feel proud when he does that, even though I shouldn't, not really. It's not my doing that we're no longer together, it's just the way it's happened.

Liberation: that's what we're all talking about.

"Do you remember walking down Zuider-Amstellaan into town?" says Papi.

"I remember walking the children to school," says Mrs. Frank suddenly.

Mr. Frank smiles. "A walk home from work!" he says.

"Running!" laughs Anne.

Margot just smiles. I wonder what she's thinking.

All through the day it comes to me. That feeling. That memory. Of walking, just walking along—not particularly going anywhere. And I smile. I can't help it. Hope is in the air. It frightens me. But I can't stop it being there. Anne and Margot smile.

Outside, the sun begins to shine again.

"Why are the British taking so long?" rages Mutti. She's strung so tight that if she let go of herself she might fly to the moon.

"They're fighting for us," I say, and it feels like a miracle again, that there are people from all over the world, fighting. Fighting to allow the differences between us. Living for us. Dying for us. Without even knowing that we're here. Will we ever see them, the British or American soldiers? And how will it happen? Will they come down the street with tanks, with flags? Will they shout, "Come out, come out, wherever you are?" Will we run down the stairs making as much noise as we can (the way Anne does sometimes when there's an air raid)? Will we stand in the sun or rain or wind again, and hold hands? Will we walk down Prinsengracht into town, and feel the air all around us, on us? "Meow!" Mouschi jumps out of my arms. I've been squeezing him.

I must stop. I must stop. Because it hurts—hoping.

"What did you do to poor Mouschi?" croons Anne as she strokes him.

"Nothing!"

"You did!" she says as she tickles him under the chin. "Didn't he? Nasty Peter." Margot turns her eyes to the ceiling, then closes them and smiles. Anne and Mouschi stare at me. What can I say? I hoped too hard. That's what I did.

"Sorry," I say.

What was it like, the liberation, when it came? I had a picture for it once. The sound of our feet running down the stairs. The feel of the air upon our faces and the sound of the bells ringing. A carillon of bells—the words that Margot used. In my picture, the leaves drifted all over us like confetti, and we threw our arms into the air and fell to the floor, or jumped into the canal. We hugged each other and we ran; we ran down the streets, through the alleyways. We screamed aloud.

Was it like that?

I don't know.

We weren't there.

Our rooms in the Annex were empty and we had gone.

AUGUST 4, 1944 — THE EIGHT IN THE ANNEX ARE BETRAYED

The moment arrives, but I am still inside and so don't see it coming.

It's hot and airless and we long to open the windows. We're studying hard. Suddenly there seems a point again. The walls are closing in, only this time it's upon them, not us.

Outside, the warehouse doors of 263 Prinsengracht are wide open onto the street. But I don't know that. We're all looking forward to it ending. The Allies are winning. We all know it. The hope beats hard inside me, a pulse, like memory returning to life. I try to stop it, but I can't. Any day now, any day, we could be free. I begin to draw the streets again. I draw the route home, all the way from Prinsengracht to Merwedeplein. In the drawings I make it autumn. I don't want to be too greedy, too hopeful.

I draw the leaves falling upon us, raining down in gold and red to celebrate. We are so close, so close, as close as the heat in the rooms behind the closed windows.

Outside.

A military vehicle draws up. A military policeman gets out. He walks toward the warehouse doors. A worker points to him and gestures upstairs, where . . . I am in my room with Mr. Frank.

"Can you see how the sentence works, Peter? In English you use the word 'it.'"

I brush the sweat out of my face and try to think.

It is about to happen, the thing we have dreaded most for two years. It is not night the way it always was in my imaginings, but morning. It's a beautiful day. The sun is shining. The birds are singing up in the leaves of the chestnut tree. Downstairs Anne is writing her diary. Margot is reading a medical textbook; she has decided she wants to be a doctor. She whispered it to me in the attic two days ago. Her eyes shone behind her glasses. "You'll be a wonderful doctor," I said.

Dr. Pfeffer is in his room writing to his Charlotte; letters full of plans. Mutti and Papi are in the kitchen, fanning themselves on the sofa. I can hear their voices, quietly talking. Everything in the Annex is calm. The moment is almost upon us now, but none of us see it coming.

At first I think it's Anne coming up the stairs, a bit too noisily, a bit too heavily. There's a noise next door, in the heat I think I hear someone say, "Raise your hands!"

There's a smothered exclamation from Mutti and a calming noise from Papi. By now Mr. Frank and I are both standing, and then they appear at the door. A Dutch man in a green uniform. He has a pistol in his hand. There are two others behind him. There was no knock; they are just here, in my room, standing in the doorway. Mr. Frank looks at me. We know immediately. We both know. It's over. The picture of hope falls to pieces inside me.

"Put your hands up!"

"Put your books away, Peter," Mr. Frank says. We look at the window, at the attic steps. There is nowhere to hide. There are three other men, all Dutch police. They make us put our hands up and they search us. We have no weapons. They push us next door. In the kitchen Mutti is standing next to Papi. They have their arms in the air.

"My family!" says Mr. Frank.

Mutti and Papi stare at us, wide eyed. None of us speak. They make us walk down the stairs.

The bookcase door that has kept us so safe and hidden is swinging loose and wide open. The sight of it is shocking. There is nowhere left to hide.

Anne is standing next to Margot, who is weeping. I stare at her. The tears fall down her face, quietly, silently. It seems impossible that Margot is crying, but she is. Anne has her foot wrapped around Margot's ankle, comforting her. She is breathing steadily, staring at the men. Mrs. Frank is on Margot's other side. They all have their hands up. A man is standing pointing a pistol at them.

"You!" he says to Mr. Frank. "Show me where you keep your jewelry and money!"

Mr. Frank points. One man rifles through the drawers. Another man returns from the Franks' bedroom with Mr. Frank's briefcase and empties it. Anne's eyes are wide. Her loose papers and diary fall out all over the floor. She breathes in. I want to hold her. Mr. Frank moves.

"Keep still!" The man stuffs our money (not much) and jewelry (not much) into the briefcase. My heart is beating very hard. Very fast. I don't know how Mr. Frank can look so calm. I think of what Mutti said: "If the liberation comes close, they'll find us. They'll shoot us. Is that what's going to happen?"

I wish it had. I wish I had died then, with Mutti beside me, but that would have been too easy. To end it then, to kill me when I still had a body and thoughts that were my own. When my hope was newly dead and still might rise.

They search through the Annex. They open cupboards and drawers. I think of the empty rooms of our old apartment, of the furniture being loaded and taken away. I know that is what will happen to us if they don't shoot us. I don't think they'll do it here. We are all sweating. It is hard to hold your hands up for very long. We look at each other and away again. We hold a conversation with our eyes. Our eyes say we are shocked. Our eyes say, *What next?*

"You may pack some clothes," the man shouts. "Quick! Quick!" We put our arms down. We go to our rooms. We don't know what to pack.

We go back downstairs. Anne is on the floor, kneeling, putting her papers into a neat pile.

"Leave them!" snaps the man. She stands up. Not quickly and not slowly. She stands up with dignity and she nods at him, as though he were worth the respect of every human being. I wish I could clap. I feel proud of her. I hope he can't see that she is shaking.

The time goes very slowly, and very fast. The leader of the police is still searching through the room.

"Is this yours?" he asks Mr. Frank, kicking a wooden chest, and suddenly his voice is different. We all look up.

"Yes, I was a reserve lieutenant in the Great War," says Mr. Frank. He sounds exactly as he always does, his voice is soft and reasonable and we all cling to it. The man stands up very straight then, and he looks at Mr. Frank differently.

"Don't hurry them!" he snaps at the other policeman.

"You should have reported that," he says to Mr. Frank, and he sounds sorry. "We could perhaps have had you sent to Theresienstadt labor camp."

"Well," says Mutti very quietly. "Perhaps we might be allowed to open a window now that everyone knows we're here?"

I look at her. She is very brave. I don't know if it has worked. I don't know if her interruption and the man's sharp "No window!" has stopped Anne and Margot noticing what's been said. Because if we're not going to a labor camp, then where are we going? We all know the words. Death camp.

"May we tidy up a little?" asks Anne, and when he nods, she kneels down again. I kneel down too. Together we gather up her diary and her papers.

"Don't worry," I whisper. "Miep'll find them, she'll save them for you, don't make them too interested in it."

"I can't leave Kitty!" she whispers.

I hold her wrist, hard. "You must," I say. "You know it has a better chance without you." The tears fill her eyes, but don't spill over. We hide the diary, under the papers, in a neat pile.

We stand up together. I can see how hard it is for her to leave the papers. I hold her hand. It's sweating. She's shaking. The wait is awful. We sit down. We can't speak. We can't believe this is happening, but we know that it is. We are allowed to have some water.

"Well," says Mutti at twelve-thirty. "Lunchtime." No one

answers, there is a silence from everyone. It is such a normal thing to say. She is crying silent tears. I could fight them, I think. I want to. I can feel my heart beating hard with it. I can feel it in Papi too. But they wouldn't just shoot *us*. They would kill all of us. Finally, at one o'clock, the van they are waiting for arrives.

"Up! Quickly!"

As we leave, one of the men kicks the papers and they scatter across the floor. Mr. Frank holds Anne close and whispers something.

We walk down the stairs. It is happening. But it's hard to believe it is happening. Mr. Kugler and Mr. Kleiman are with us. We are sorry about that. The police are in front and behind.

Outside.

We step through the door.

We are outside.

It is so bright. So bright and sharp; the daylight after the dark. It burns my eyes. We look at each other. We all look different. We look so white in the light. All of us stop for a moment in front of the truck. I hold my face up to the light and feel it on my skin. It is so warm, the air. So soft and so wonderful.

"Get in!"

I open my eyes. We are all doing the same thing, standing in the air of the outside with our faces turned up to the sun. It is just a moment, less than a second. And then it's over.

"I said, get in!"

The truck has no windows. Inside it is hot and dark and we begin to fear where we are going.

PART 2:

The Camps

MAY 1945 — PETER: MAUTHAUSEN, SICK BAY

So we have arrived—the moment is here, it is now.

I am lying in a bunk in Mauthausen.

There is word I must remember. A word that stains all it touches—a word that can never mean just a place, or be just a word. It is a word without hope or desire— Auschwitz.

I think I must be alive. But I'm not sure.

Am I alive or am I dead? How can I know—because they are the same thing for a Jew in Auschwitz.

It was there they sent us to first.

In Auschwitz we had dreams, and when we woke the dream went on—and it was a nightmare.

I'm dying. I must be.

Everyone who has been there is dead—even when they are still walking.

And now it's my turn.

How can I speak of this—are there words?

And will you listen now the time has come?

Will you go on, as I am forced to, turning the pages of each day—one after the other—and surviving?

Because this is not a story. This is the truth. These things really happened.

This is what all of us here long for you, outside, to know.

That we went gently, most of us. We walked into the night of the camps in long lines not knowing where we were going. We went in trains, wearing all of our possessions like hope. Once, we were legion, now we are few.

Now our naked bodies lie in piles. Our bones are ground to dust and we are . . . ashes.

That is the truth.

———

I am so sorry to have to ask again, but is anybody there?

Is anybody listening?

Are there any of us left?

Or is it just me still breathing?

Am I the last—alone—in this river of dead and putrid bodies lying all around me?

I want to shout, to ask if anyone else is lying here like me, still breathing. But they might hear me, might come, might shoot me.

And someone must survive.

"Survive, be brave," whispers Papi.

"Tell," whispers Mr. Frank, "tell our story . . ."

The bodies around me are beginning to smell.

Is it really happening? The dream we all had, over and over

and over. Is everyone dead? Are there no Jews left except me?
Outside, there are no shouts, no guards, no music. I close my
eyes.

"Survive, be brave," whispers Papi.

But I am not brave. And I am tired.

"Tell, tell, tell, tell, tell," the voices beat at my body, so many
voices, so many bodies, so many stories ended, I cannot tell
them all. I am the wrong person. It should be Anne here, Anne
with her shining eyes standing in the doorway of my bedroom.
Anne smiling. Anne laughing. Anne crying: "I have so much to
say, so many stories inside of me, Peter!"

"How can I tell of this?" I ask her in despair.

"Put it into words," she whispers, "and begin."

"Are there words for this?"

"What else have we?"

And so I begin.

First they took us to Westerbork, a holding camp. I remember
Anne, her eyes dancing in the light of outside. We were still
all together then. We still had hope. The Allies were coming,
heading toward Holland. It was a race against time. Every
Tuesday the trains came and went again.

Where did they go?

They went east:
to Theresienstadt,
to Sobibor,
to Bergen-Belsen
and to Auschwitz.

There was a river of us walking, a river of us lying, a river of us working— a river of us dying.

"Oh, Anne! Where are the words for this?"

"Inside you," she whispers. "Just find them—begin."

They put us on a train.

I am on a train. I do not know where we are going.

Auschwltz, Auschwitz. In my memory the wheels click it, whisper it, taunt me with the name of our destination. Auschwitz, Auschwitz, Auschwitz. But my memory is wrong. We did not know where we were going.

We have everything with us, the few things that remain. The doors close. Suddenly there is no light—or just a sliver of it, like a half-memory, high up in the carriage.

We can hear each other breathe in the dark. There is a sudden silence and in it we all hear a noise, the scratching of the chalk on the side of the car. They are writing a number—the number of us inside.

"Are they going to lose us?" somebody says. A few laugh. It's the afternoon. There are whistles and noise, palms bang against the door. Guards shout, and then the train starts to move. We are jolted to one side. We reach out to each other to steady ourselves. I hold on to Anne. The memory of her body against mine in the attic is sudden and sharp. We let go.

The wheels click a rhythm. I can feel my eyes closing; my head begins to fall. I jerk awake, come to. The light has gone and it is dark. Beyond the heat of our bodies it's cold—but still the train keeps moving.

Somebody groans. We are all thinking the same. When will it stop? When can we let go? Of our bladders, our eyes, our bodies—still standing. There is no noise, just the warm sharp smell of fresh piss rising, a groan of relief. Over and over, until the stench is as thick as a coat covering us.

"Sorry," the whispered words come. "Sorry, I'm so very sorry."

Now no one can rest on the floor.

We stand, hoping that soon we will stop. Sometimes the train slows, our heads rise up from their half slumber and wait, but the train goes on. We lean against the walls, against each other. We rock with the motion of the wheels, not noticing we're moving. Holding on to each other, to our bladders. Soon. We hope it will be soon that we arrive.

We did not know what we were hoping for.

The sun rises. The train keeps on going. People give up, they lie in the piss, they lie on top of each other.

Mutti puts her coat down on the floor. It gives us a patch to sit on. We are lucky. We take turns to sit on it. We piss on the floor, facing outward. We have not had to shit yet.

In my doze I hear the train wheels click. I wake up. This time it isn't a dream. The train slows and stops.

"Where? Where are we going?" someone calls. A tall man stares through the slit in the side of the carriage. He reads out Polish names. Inside there are groans. Silence. The smell of fear—and the sudden stink of shit.

"If it's like the camp at Westerbork, it won't be so bad!" whispers Anne. Nobody answers. We all know it won't be like Westerbork—that was just a holding camp. She begins to shiver. Someone begins to wail: "I can't wake her. I can't wake her." Someone else mutters, "She's the lucky one."

People bang on the door. "Let us out!"

Mr. Frank begins to whisper. "Stay together. Whatever happens we must stay together. Remember. They are losing.

The end is coming. Wherever we end up, we must let people know that. We have information. We can give them hope."

He was right. Stupid us. We gave it away for nothing.

Somewhere in the cattle truck someone begins to say the Kaddish—the prayer for the dead. The train begins to move.

Day three. More people start to shit themselves. The smell makes others vomit.

Us men stand together with our backs to the crowd. We hold each other. We brace ourselves against the moving walls. We try to protect our space.

I feel Anne's hair beneath my chin.

"I'm so thirsty, Peter!" she whispers.

"I know," I say.

It's getting harder to stand. Sometimes now, the train stops.

For hours.

"Water!" people cry. "Water!" But there is no water. No one answers. There is just the heat. The stench. The silence. Outside, one voice calls to another on the platform.

"Answer us!" the man near the slit shouts. "Answer us, you bastards!"

We wait, but there is no answer.

"We are people, people in here," Anne whispers. But they do not answer, as though we really *are* cattle, lowing, calling out in a strange inhuman speech.

Beyond understanding.

The train starts again. The wheels click. The train rocks on its way.

It stops again. It is dark and we have stopped so many times before, we are used to it now. We think it will go on forever. Until we die. Some already have.

We are lost, in time passing without measure. We are awake and not awake. We are alive and not alive when the train finally stops—and the doors open.

Are there words even for this, Anne?

"*Yes, even for this,*" she whispers. "*You must go back there, Peter, so you can find them.*"

The light is blinding after the soft dark of the carriages. Voices shout. "*Raus! Raus! Schnell! Schnell! Schnell!*"

The fresh air hits the carriage and makes the smell even worse. We are suddenly ashamed. We stink and cower, try to hide ourselves. People fall and jump and crawl out of the carriage onto the platform.

We are the only ones left now. Us eight, standing in the doorway, staring.

There are men in stripes. Jews, like us. But not like us. Shorn. Like the walking dead, they are shouting at us in the lit-up, searchlight dark.

So much light.

"Out! Out!" they scream, and the dogs bark. Anne steps back.

"Women and children left!" Anne starts to move left. I pull her back. I want her close. We're still in the carriage. "Men, right. Women, here!" "Left!" "Right!" We hold hands and stare. And then I realize. The words make sense because they're speaking German. I can understand them.

An old man stands on the platform, staring, not moving. He doesn't understand. He stares around him, lost, pushing his glasses up his nose.

"Didn't you hear me?" a guard shouts. He strikes the man in the face. We stare, our eyes aren't big enough, our hearts not wide enough to take this in—to understand.

"I said *left*, you fool!"

The old man shakes his head, there is blood in his eyes, he can't see. He holds his hands up helplessly. The guard strikes him and steps over his fallen body. Dr. Pfeffer steps forward. Mr. Frank pulls him rapidly back. The guard steps up to the next man—perhaps he is the old man's son, I don't know. It's all so fast and calm that I'm still not sure I saw it. The man doesn't say anything, he punches the

guard so hard his head rocks back and we all hear a snap.
The guard stumbles, the man stands, fists bunched waiting to fight. The guard recovers his balance and shoots him.
On the floor of the platform the old man wails. They shoot
him too.

The shaved skeletons in stripes bend down and begin to
search the dead men's pockets. I wonder why they open their
mouths to search inside. After the silence and smell of the
carriage the sound of the commands feels deafening.

But in my memory it is all silent. Flashes of searchlit moments.
Pictures like guns going off. Memories of words that make no
sense. The sound of a language that I recognize—but don't yet
truly understand.

"You!" The guard means us. We step down. "Left, left, left."
We men have stepped forward, determined to protect. I am
holding Mutti's hand.

"No! Women this side! Right! I said *right!*"

We stare at each other but not for long. We are shocked.
We are scared. We are so tired and thirsty we cannot think.
We cannot take it in. We have seen that they'll kill us if we
do not do whatever they want—and quickly. We glance at
each other before we let go of each other's hands like obedi-
ent children.

It is only a moment—a fraction of time, but later it will haunt us. How we seemed to let go of each other so easily.

"Peter!"

"Mutti!"

"Peter!"

"Anne!"

We hold each other with our eyes and then they disappear—into the dark.

Are they alive? Are they dead? Have they known this horror too?

I don't know. They are led away from us. We glance up and they are gone. So fast we never even noticed.

"This way! This way!" We are marched off. You can probably smell us coming from a mile away.

They march us through the black, wide gates.

ARBEIT MACHT FREI.

Work brings freedom.

That is what the gates say.

There was a rumor that in one camp they hung a dead Jew up on the black iron, a fresh one every day. We all believed it. We believed it because we knew by then that it was possible. We

286

didn't comment, we just grunted and carried on, putting one foot in front of the other.

They put us in a room. We stare at each other. What has happened? We know something has, but what? The lights are very bright. People mutter: what will happen now? Somewhere, someone is praying over and over in a wail. "What good is that?" I snarl.

"It's helping him, Peter!" Mr. Frank's voice is soft. Unchanging. I shut up. We smell. We smell like animals. And our faces are puffed up and strange with the need for water.

A man comes in. "Take everything off. Leave it all here. You can have it back later."

I look around. We all have the same look: confused, dumb, scared. Made similar by our hunger and thirst and separation.

By the end you could not even tell if we were men or women. In the end we are all bones. All bones. As I am.

"Please! Water! We're thirsty!" says one man.

"Later," says the German.

Slowly we undress. We try not to look at each other. There is an old man. He has glasses. "These too?" he asks.

"I said everything!" He is talking as though we are ill, or sick. He is talking as though we are children. It is confusing. He is not angry. I don't understand it. Why is he behaving as though this is normal? Why are we? We are standing before him desperate, and cold, and thirsty and hungry—still believing that if we get it right we can survive.

"Remove everything!" he says again.

"But without his glasses my father can't see!"

"Then he is not of much use to us, is he?" the man says.

The men in stripes come in. They search through our clothes, separating, removing. I think of the crows that gather in the chestnut tree.

We hold our hands to cover ourselves. We look down. We feel the shame is ours. I have never seen my father or Dr. Pfeffer or Mr. Frank naked. We cannot meet each other's eyes. We cannot look anywhere except at the floor.

They take us to the showers. They are hot. We can't believe it. The wonder of being able to wash off the fear and stink and terror of that journey. It gives us hope.

"Why would they do all this if they were just going to kill us?" asks Dr. Pfeffer.

"Who are the Jews in the stripes?" whispers another. But we have no answers.

We are shaved. The men who do it wear green triangles.

Green triangle meant criminal. They gave criminals razors to
shave us with.

We stand in a line. We watch. We sit. They shave all of us.
Everything. Our heads. Our arms. Our privates. And I know
we are all thinking the same thing. What about our women? Is
this happening to them too? It hurts. Some men cry silently.

They'll get used to it. Or die.
   It happens every week: on Saturday.

I look at the men who do this to us. Who are they? *Are some*
of them really Jewish? I keep thinking. The thought goes
around and around in my mind: *How can they be?* What is
happening if they are Jewish? Is this real?

How strange, to think that I tried to make sense of it, that we
all did, as though that were possible.

We are naked and shivering. There are no towels to dry ourselves with. Our clothes and shoes have gone, and in their
place are piles of the pajamas. Striped, like the men's who
have shaved and stripped us. We don't want them. There are
no shoes—there is only a huge pile of clogs.

The old man cries out: "I want my glasses, I can't see without my glasses!"

"Your glasses are gone," says the German calmly. He makes a gesture; one of the striped men strikes the man across the face.

Already it doesn't surprise me. I turn away. We put on the stripes. We try to find clogs that fit.

"Get a good fit, it's important," says Papi, and Dr. Pfeffer agrees. "Shoes are the difference between life and death," he says. We grab armfuls of the clogs, try them all and grab more, keeping the best to try again. Some of the men look at us like we're mad.

Those were the ones who died quickly.

Others join us in a frantic hunt.

They lasted longer.

We stand up, the four of us. And we look at each other. We look away, quickly. We look like them now. The Jews in the stripes, who speak that strange, harsh language—and beat and kick and kill us. When we try to walk we find we cannot lift our feet, and so we hobble, as they do, for fear of the clogs falling off.

It is done.

We have become Häftlinge.

We are not sure what has happened. But we know something has.

It is called Auschwitz.

It is called death camp.

But they are not finished. Not yet. They raise my sleeve and a sharp pain pierces my wrist. What is it? I look down. There is a number: B-9286.

I am no longer Peter van Pels.

I am Stegi Stersi, B-9286.

Look, if I turn my wrist I can still see it.

Our clothes have gone, our hair has gone   our names have gone.

We are numbers now.

Numbers on the side of a cattle car, blue numbers tattooed upon a wrist.

It is done.

We have crossed the gates into a human hell.

We are in Auschwitz.

The memories crowd now—as thick and heavy as the dead.
Why did I let go of Mutti's hand so easily? I didn't know what
was happening. There was no time to think.

"Petel!" She said my name, and then she was gone. They were all gone, our women. Into the chimneys of this hell. I let go of her. I let go of everything in the end.

Even myself.

But not yet.

Let me tell you.

Let me tell you.

If anybody is there?

If anybody is listening?

In those first minutes the seconds felt like hours. We sat shaved and uniformed and numbered. Häftlinge now, unable to wake to the shock of that final parting we didn't even know had happened, yet sensed within us—a severing from our women, from ourselves—the first of many to come as we are kicked, or beaten or hanged or shot, or taken into the showers that turn water into gas. There are so many ways to part with life.

Those of us who learned quickly, despite the shock, we might survive. But even we, who spoke German, we didn't really understand. How could we? How can we?

Do you?

Even now when it is nearly over, it makes no sense to me.

Can it really make sense to the Germans?

Why is it me who feels such shame?

Shame that I fought for my life, and watched others die.

Shame that I did nothing to save them.

It haunts me as I lie here, waiting to die. The structure of the camps, the bones that held them up, are within me—written in invisible ink—engraved on me like the blue tattoo on my wrist.

And will never let me go.

"How can I tell of this, Anne?"

"You must put one word in front of the other and walk with them, as we have walked through this, Peter, with no thought of tomorrow."

"But there is no one to hear."

"Then write it on air, they cannot burn ideas."

"I will. I will walk with my memories toward you."

I am scared.

I am alone.

I am the last Jew.

The guard is screaming at us.

"Stand in fives! Fives! I said fives! Are you men or morons?"

Mr. Frank gathers us, begins to explain, in Dutch, in English, in French, in any language that might help us understand what it is that we have to do. The guard sneers at him: "A professor, are you? Your type never lasts long!"

Mr. Frank doesn't answer; he obeys, and fast. He understands, look busy. Bow your head. Our first *Appel*—roll call—our first lesson in how to be Häftlinge.

"Stand in fives, two yards apart!"

Mr. Frank translates, we listen, watch, and copy; already anxious not to be the one who is hit, the one who falls and might be shot.

We used to laugh at him, me and Anne, at his poor Dutch accent. Dutch is no good to us here. It is German that will save us, if we can be saved.

"Is it really German?" I whisper. Because although I understand the words, it is nothing like the German *we* speak.

"Of a kind," he replies, quietly. He is calm. I can see him now standing before us, bigger than the uniform they put us in.

In that moment he is like the one word you can understand in a foreign language. The word you cling to as though it could explain the whole sentence.

Help me, I think. *Help me.*

Because even standing in the searchlights looking like Häftling, I still had the smell of freedom on my skin. The belief that there was such a thing as understanding this. A child's belief that somewhere, elsewhere, the world might go on making sense.

Mr. Frank changes the brutal sound of the bitten-off German into slow, clear sentences for us, and we obey him. We stand in fives. Two yards apart. We learn our lesson. For a moment he looks startled as we shuffle into shape. As though it is him who is making this happen.

We don't know yet that we will do this every day and every evening.

We will stand an arm's length apart from our neighbor, in a straight line of five, and make it easy for them to count us.

I will stand in snow and rain. In fog and mist. In sun and dust. In hail.

I will be one of a five, that is one of a ten, that is one of a hundred, a thousand, a million. How many of us have been counted and how many times?

I don't know.

I will shuffle on my blistered and breaking feet in and out of the gate, in lines. In rows.

Sometimes I will stand for hours, my head bowed against the cold and driving snow, because there is a gap in the line, or because today the guard feels like it. I do not wonder why, I stand and wait and endure.

For hours.

Sometimes people fall beside me. They might be sent to

the sick bay, or they might be shot where they lie. I learn to stay standing.

Once, we stood in rows and watched a man hang. It was cold. We dropped our heads and wished that it was over so that we could stop standing.

"Do it quickly!" the young Pole next to me whispered. He wanted to be out of the shivering cold, to get through the day to come. He was already longing for the short break and the watery soup. His words came from the ache in his legs and the cold through his shirt.

Dammit, hurry up and let me get out of this cold, get on with surviving, finishing this step, this day, this night, this roll call.

They shouted at us to put our heads up and watch him die.

"*Haben Sie verstanden?*" they shouted. "Have you understood?" And we all knew what we had to reply.

"*Jawohl!*" But they never asked us what we had understood.

Our shame. That's what.

And their hatred.

"Comrades, I am free," the condemned man shouted as he put the noose over his own head—and jumped before they could push him.

There was only one road to freedom in Auschwitz.

To choose the manner of your death.

I wish I'd died that way too. Alive. Fighting. Standing in front of our unbowed heads, our eyes staring up at him through the gray cold. That man will be remembered. He will be counted. He will not be one of us. One of the millions like gray striped rats, dying in piles. Well, I say that now. But then I just wanted the standing to be over. I could only think of the cold and the need to move. Of the moment when the dreadful music that played as we shuffled in and out of the gates would finally stop.

And the roll call would be over.

For a while I worked in the postal department, in the warm, where I sorted their post. Where I could get extra rations of bread.

Why did I get that job? Who knows? Maybe because I looked German. Maybe because I walked past at the right time.

There is no why in this world, haven't I explained that?

Don't you get it yet? Must you be beaten too? Must you be made to eat soup from a bowl standing up?

"You smell like animals!" That's what they said.

Yes, we are like animals. We eat fast and standing up. We lick our bowls, searching for every last morsel. If there is food we will snatch it, fight for it. We are the beasts of your burden, your hate. We think like animals, of simple things.

Food.

Warmth.

Sleep.

But we are not animals.

Animals do not fear death, or anonymity, or a story untold.

So I am not an animal, do you hear me?

Even if you replace my name with a number, give me no spoon to eat with, or clothes, or shoes to walk in—so that I am forced to live and eat like one. I am not an animal.

Although even now I am waiting.

Waiting for the command to come at me through this sleeping, waking, dreaming nightmare. Through the cold, ball-breaking dark of a winter dawn, and the harsh early light of summer. The word that breaks me in half and forces this body to wake to a day my mind cannot make sense of.

Wystawach.

Wake up.

And I know that when I hear it, despite everything, I will try to rise, to get up, to stand, and wait to be counted. The command is wired into me.

Wystawach.

Wake up.

And I cannot escape it.

"How can I tell of this?"

"Because you must," whispers Anne.

But is it possible for you, outside, to understand, even if the words exist?

Do we even have the same language? Here is a plate, I say. There is a bowl. These are easy words, but there are others more difficult. This is where your world stops and mine begins.

Can you cross the space between us?

To hear the meaning of a word.

"Say it," whispers Anne.

"But why?"

"Because it is words that make man free—not work."

Seleckcja.

Seleckcja.

That is what they call it—the thing that happens. We have never heard the word, although we have already, all unknowingly, survived that first selection on the station platform. We are the high numbers in the camp, the new ones—the stupid and clumsy and dangerous.

Dangerous because we don't know the rules, we draw attention to ourselves with our awkward shuffle. We trip over our clogs and bring others down with us.

We are hated.

Seleckcja.

It is October. The word whispers its way around the huts of Auschwitz, hangs like a hawk above us, waiting to descend. There are too many of us. The low numbers know it, they sense what's coming, the old hands. And they whisper the word—*seleckcja*.

Seleckcja.

They look at us with hate. We've made this happen, us high numbers, turning up and causing crowding. There are too many of us and now the guards will have to do something about it. They forget that it's not us killing them—not us who think they are not people but numbers.

Seleckcja.

I look at Papi, he shakes his head.

"Well. At least we're inside!" he says. We were living in tents, but the wind has blown them away. We sleep sideways now, four to a bunk.

No, we didn't sleep. That was not sleep. There should be another word for it, that thing we did with our eyes closed, our minds playing over and over, trying to make sense of the impossible. Fending off the grunt and the knee in the back, the grinding of

someone else's imagined food in our ears, the descent into a
dream, without warning. A perfect carrot, whole from
the ground, it is nearly in my mouth, my spit is wet with the
anticipation of it, my teeth can feel the crunch of something
solid at last beneath them . . . I wake . . . the dream spreads . . .
my mouth is empty, my spit sour . . . it takes a few seconds to
dawn . . . to the word that pulls us from this place that is not
sleep.

WYSTAWACH.

Wake up!

The Blockaltester shouts and another day begins.

There is a new fear in the air—not the daily fear of living or
dying, of the cold, or the pain of walking on blistered feet
and the whipping . . .

Death is coming. It is always coming, but now it is closer.

It does not matter if you are young or old, healthy or
ill, if you are Dutch or Greek or even German. All that
matters is that you are a Jew—and even one of you is
too many.

"There are too many of us," says Mr. Frank. "They are
choosing who will die."

We know it's true. It doesn't shock us—it makes as much
sense as anything else that's happening.

"We're all dying," says Papi. "It's just a matter of timing!" And then he laughs. I stare at him, but Mr. Frank laughs out loud. The others stare, his laughter sounds shocking and huge, like remembering something forgotten.

"Quiet!" shouts the Blockaltester.

And we obey.

We know it's going to happen. We are going to be selected. But we don't know how. Dr. Pfeffer has disappeared. Mr. Frank asks questions, but there are no answers. Men shrug or shake their heads. "Up in smoke," suggests one low number. Mr. Frank puts his head in his hands. "Somehow I only really got to know him in here," he whispers. That night another man lies where Dr. Pfeffer was.

"Watch," says Mr. Frank. "Whatever happens, keep your eyes on the low numbers; copy them. Look like you know what you're doing."

Rumors are rife. It will only be the young who are chosen. It will only be the old. It won't be our section, but another camp. For once it will not be us Jews, this time it will be the criminals.

We knew somewhere inside ourselves that it was not true. We were doing our own choosing, pretending that it will be you. Not me. What else could we do when . . . ?

There is no escape. Nowhere to run to, except for the wire, but that is only for the brave—those who understand that there is only one choice: and the choice is not *who* will die, but *how* to die. And so they choose to die in the only way left to them—on the wire.

Do you understand?
    Can you?
    That it was not an act of despair.
    But an act of life.

For the rest of us, we say the words we don't believe to each other. That it will not be us this time, but someone else, somewhere else. We allow the words to flatten the fear surrounding us, to soften the threat hanging in the air above us like ashes.

It is that or the wire. There is no in-between. No other way.

Seleckcja.

We are showered. Shaved. Disinfected. We are prepared for another week. But today is different; today the bell goes. That means we must go to our huts. Everything stops. Around the square, conversations end, the bartering over spoons and shoes and bread falters. There is silence. Dealers put away their wares. And now even those last few who hadn't somehow sensed it would happen know it now.

It is time. We will be chosen. We will be selected.

We stop what we are doing and go into the huts.

I am given a card. I stare at it in my hand. It has my name on it. Peter van Pels. It has my age and the date I was born. It reminds me of something I had forgotten. It reminds me of who I am.

I put it away. The low numbers have not looked at theirs. They have not been caught out by the sight of themselves written down—by the memory of who they are.

They hold it tight, check quickly, just once, that it is right, and look away.

"Strip!"

I'm used to the sight of our naked bodies now. I'm not ashamed anymore. I fold the clothes up on my bunk, and put my clogs on top.

"They'll be waiting for you when you get back," says the low number who sleeps beneath me. And he's right. Nobody takes the chance to steal anything. The extra bread anyone has is shared, not bartered. None of us knows who will be coming back.

We wait in the huts. Some sleep. Some pray. Most of us stare, lost into the distance. Our minds slip from underneath us, try to spare us the horror. I'm not scared now. Now that it's finally here, I am calm.

Yes, that's right. That's right. No feeling can last forever, how else could we endure? Even fear can only last so long before it is beaten into submission.

We were quiet.

It comes suddenly, even though we're waiting for it. The noise and shouting and screaming of the Blockaltesters breaks us out of our calm, out of whatever world we've made inside ourselves to contain this horror. It drives us up off the bunks and naked, out into the freezing air . . . out into another room where we are crammed in tight, pressed together . . . waiting . . . us high numbers are not sure what we are waiting for. Slowly the pressure begins to ease. I remember Mr. Frank's words. I watch. I am nearly at the door now. I choose a low number to watch. He is old but that doesn't matter. I watch him. I watch him as he gets closer to the door. I watch him lift his body up on his hips and throw his bony chest out. I watch him run as fast as he can with his knees up high and his arms pumping.

And then it is my turn.

In front of me there is a yard, at the end of it there is another door. Beside the door there are guards and an SS man. I face them. I hold my head up. I lift my knees. I throw my chest out. I run as fast as I can. I hope that they will choose me to live. I give the SS man my card.

It's over.

We go back to the hut. We dress. Everybody crowds around the old, the weak, the ill, and the lame.

All kindness and calm is gone.

"Left or right? Left or right?" they say. "Which way did your card go?"

"Left!" they say, and again. "Left." "Left." "Left."

"Did you look?" asks Papi, quietly. "Did you see which way your card went?" Because it's obvious now that all the cards that went left are the selected.

I shake my head. I didn't know. I didn't know that's what you had to do. I'm ashamed. I didn't look closely enough, follow carefully enough.

"Did you?" I ask. Papi shakes his head, and then he smiles.

"No!" he says.

And then the soup arrives.

"Look," says Papi. "They've given me double. Here, Petel, you must have it."

Why? Why have they given him more? I look around. He's not the only one. All the Musselmänner: the weak, the old, the useless. They've all got double, all the men whose cards were on the left. I look at Papi.

He has been selected.

"No!" I say. "You have it." But he won't.

"Please, Peter, or Mutti will kill me. Imagine!"

But I shake my head. I can't. Even though I am so hungry.

No, I was not hungry. Hungry is a word that you can understand. This hunger is not in my stomach, it is in my skin—my bones. If you cut my legs off they would walk toward a bowl of soup without me.

I want my father's soup, but I can't eat it.

I lie in my bunk at night, awake. I feel the knees in my back and the filthy breath we all have in my face. Voices scream and shout in the dark. They curse and groan and wail and whisper with hurt and longing and fear and all the feelings that lie dead during the day, while we fight for survival. They rise up out of the mouths of the sleeping.

I can't sleep. I lie awake and listen.

My eyes are still wide open when dawn comes.

"*Wystawach,*" shouts the Blockaltester.

But I am already awake.

———

The next day everything is the same. Roll call. Work detail. We wake. We work. It is lager-cold. We are lager-hungry. Only one thing is different—Papi gets another extra ration of soup.

"They're fattening me up for something!" he jokes. We glance at each other and away. I touch his arm. His fingertips brush my face. He knows. We both know.

"Please," he says quietly, "eat it, it will keep you going."

That is what Mutti always said to us in winter, when she gave us porridge. The words burn us. Touch us in that private place called the past that we must not remember, must keep dead or frozen if we are to survive. We look at each other. He smiles.

"Petel," he says, "please." Slowly he hands me the bowl. I raise it to my mouth. It is barely warm, but it burns me so that I can hardly swallow.

"That's right," he says, "get it down you." And he watches each mouthful, not knowing that his own mouth moves with mine until every last morsel has gone. And then he puts his hand on my shoulder.

"Well done," he says. And he pats my shoulder. "Well done."

I lean against him, and for a moment I feel his body warm against mine and know that he is here. And then I stand up straight.

"We must all do difficult things to survive," he says. And he smiles again. He holds my face in the palms of his hands and stares at it. It is only for a second.

"Be brave. Survive," he says, and then he lets go of me. He eats nothing more. He gives me all his bread and soup.

They take them early, while they are working. We have said goodbye. We are lucky. Mr. Frank did not have that. Later that afternoon we see a cart full of their empty clothes come back and know that it is done. Mr. Frank puts his hand on my shoulder. We don't say anything. There is nothing that can be said.

But I am different afterward.

Now do you understand the meaning of the word?

Seleckcja.

After that I was no longer Peter. I was Stegi Stersi, B-9286 Häftling. Untermensch. A creature of the lager. A creature who would do anything to keep alight the morsel of life that his father fed with soup.

Be brave. Survive.

That is what I have done.

For him.

Whatever it costs.

I killed kindness. I stole. If we needed more bread I got it. There was no other way. A nail loose in the floorboards, an empty sack, a spoon: I stood near the latrines and sold whatever we found.

I learned Greek: *klepsiklepsi*. Here there's no need for grammar. I learned enough—enough to buy and sell and barter.

And survive.

I did it like this.

From the first sight of the old man I gave him a week. He had Musselman written all over him. A week to go before he was dead, and then *they* got all the gold in his mouth. What a waste. I had to be quick, and I had to be lucky. He was in the bunk below. But we'd all seen that flash in his mouth. We were all onto him. I sat with him.

"There are ways to learn. To survive," I said. He tried to nod.

"My wife," he whispered.

"Afterward. You can't think about her now."

He had that look. The one we all had when we arrived. Of pain and confusion. The look that all of us hate, that none of us want to remember, the look that makes us cruel and harsh.

"My wife!" He shakes his head. "Where's my wife?" The boy in the bunk across laughs. "You're not at home now!" he spits out. It's what we all say to the high numbers. Why are they so stupid?

"Forget about your wife," I say. "I can get you bread."

"Bread?" he asks again. I want to hit him, he's so slow. My God, he thinks he will be *given* things.

"I'll help you," I say. "Give me that gold in your mouth and I'll get you a spoon, a bowl, bread. You need these things to survive."

Did I say they never gave us bowls or spoons? We had to pay for them with bread, or soup or whatever we could find, and yet to barter was illegal.

He stares at me, shaking his head. I'd like to rip the gold right out of his mouth.

"You'll die without extra food!" I say, but he shakes his head. "My wife!" he says again.

"Fine!" I say. "You'll see!"

He's put on work detail. Two days later he offers me his tooth. I do a deal with a civilian and get twenty rations of bread. Twenty! Spread out over a whole month. I share it with him and Mr. Frank. But even that can't keep the Musselmän alive. He's dead within a week.

That's how I survived.

I sell anything I can. And if the Blockaltester is eager, I sell to him too. And then we get soup from the bottom of the pot, sometimes with vegetables.

Once I got a tiny piece of sausage. Do you know what I did? I put it in my mouth. And kept it there. It made the soup taste. And at night I chewed it. And swallowed it. A piece of meat. That was a good day.

Now do you get it? This is what I did. This is how I lasted. For some of us survival was luck. No, for all of us it was luck. But for most of us it was because we learned to cheat and lie and steal and stand by—and watch while others were beaten and died.

In this way they etched their hatred upon us.

But still we dreamed.

Of telling someone, anyone—you—that it is happening.

But even our dreams failed us.

I dream of Anne. We are not in the attic, we're in the branches of the chestnut tree—outside. I can feel the branches beneath me, and the breeze in my face. The air runs like the sound of water through the leaves. The sun shines.

I am happy.

Anne stares at me with her bright brown eyes, her head bent like a bird. Happiness drifts up in me like leaves.

I am telling her everything. Everything. The words fall out of me.

I tell her how I can't sleep: of the hunger, of the fear, of how they beat us and starve us—of how even the work they make us do is not real. That sometimes we spend days moving wood from one end of a site to the other, and tomorrow, back again. I tell her of the chambers that gas us, and the ovens that burn us. The selections . . . and Anne listens and nods, and in her hands is her diary. I watch her hand writing, writing it all down as I speak.

I feel my words go in through her eyes and down onto the page, and a great weight leaves my body. I am full of joy.

I am a leaf, a bird, a balloon—a thing that can fly and float away.

I am grateful.

"Anne!" I whisper her name, reach out to touch her, to be sure that she is real. She moves away.

Anne looks up at me, but her eyes are blank as she smiles and begins to climb down the tree.

"Anne!" I shout, but she doesn't answer. Her diary lies on the branch beside me. I reach for it. I open it. I stare at it. I flick through the pages, backwards, forward, hope fading inside me, because no matter how I search . . . the pages are empty . . .

I open my eyes. The noise is all around me, the noise of men chewing on their dreams.

On emptiness.

By day we were made animals. But in our dreams we couldn't stop hoping that someone, somewhere, might hear us.

Are you there?

Are you listening?

We know we might not last.

That our story might be stolen.

And so we fight to survive.

I robbed, I stole.

I lied.

I did all I could. Became what I must.

To be brave and survive.

Can you hear me?

Because I must tell.

All of it.

I did everything.

I did anything . . .

I deserted Otto Frank.

I left him in Auschwitz.

I betrayed the man who tried to save me.
It was winter then.
Winter in Auschwitz.

The Allies are coming. Sometimes the planes fly overhead. The bones of the camp are finally breaking. Who will escape through the cracks?

I am scared.

They are gathering us together. They are going to march us somewhere. Away from the planes and the Allies, away from freedom.

"What shall I do?"

"Stay!" says Mr. Frank. "The Allies are nearly here. Hide, Peter. This is our chance!"

But what if they find me? What if they shoot the ill and useless before they leave? Or gas them? That's what they've always done. That's what they will do again—won't they?

"Stay!" says Mr. Frank, but he is so thin that he will never make it on a march. To stay is his only chance. I stare at him.

"I'm scared," I say.

"I know," he says. "Stay, Peter! Hide. Liberation is coming!" He is old now, his cheeks stick to his bones. We stare at each other. He *has* to stay—and they will kill him. That's what I think. They will kill all of the ones who cannot work, they always have. If he stays he will be killed. If I stay I will be killed with him.

I must decide.

In the end it is quick. I am rounded up with the others. We do not get the chance to say goodbye.

I am walking. I put one foot in front of the other. The air is freezing. We are outside the gates. The sky is gray. The earth is hard and cold against my feet. It is winter. I watch my feet moving. I do not look up. I put one foot in front of the other. Right foot, left foot.

I have left him. I have left him behind, the last of us. I have deserted him. Because I want to live. Right foot, left foot. Right foot, left foot.

When I finally look up, the day is nearly done. There are fewer of us. They have shot the ones who fell, who could not keep up. On a hillside there are trees. The sight of them makes my heart leap up. They are green. Fir trees. The color burns bright against my eyes. I am not used to it. Color.

We sleep where we fall. In the morning we leave the dead where they are. Frozen and curled in their blanket of frost.

We walk. We put one foot in front of the other.

I have left him. I have left him behind. Each step takes me farther, and farther from him.

I walk for days, I see villages again, and people who are not guards, or Häftlinge. I see a woman wearing a bright blue scarf on her head. I cannot stop staring at it, it is so beautiful. She offers us food. The Häftling who takes her food is shot.

"What can I do for them?" she asks, shocked.

"Nothing," say the guards.

Her kindness confuses us. Feelings flare up and burn in us. Die because they cannot be borne.

I am walking.

I have shed everything. One by one the people I have loved are gone. I am alone. I am walking bones—and soon now, it will be over.

Soon, even the smoke will stop coming out of the chimneys, the last pieces of bone will have been ground to dust and they will have won. They will blow the last of our dust away upon the wind, and in the years that follow even their stories will be true.

That we were only as they saw us:

Rats. Cockroaches. Crushed.

And so we few that remain go on. We put one foot in front of the other. We walk. When we stumble and fall and want to die, we get up—and go on. Because this is all there is. There is no Peter, no number.

There is only survival.

Them or us.

Their story or ours.

Which will it be?

Can you hear me?

Or is it just like in my dreams?

Are you already turning and walking away, back into the sunlight of that other world—your world—where I no longer exist?

Am I truly the last?

The last Jew on earth?

There is a noise outside the hut. I close my eyes. Footsteps. I lie still, hoping they will think I am dead. The footsteps keep on coming. They are searching through the bodies, looking for signs of life.

"I think they're all dead," a voice says.

Someone is standing beside my bed.

"I think there's life in this one!"

I do not move. If I am lucky I will not be worth a bullet. I would like to die without that final violence.

"Can you hear me?" the voice says into my ear. "Who are you?"

He is speaking in Spanish. He repeats the words in German. "Who are you?"

I open my eyes. The man is not dressed as a guard. He is thin, but not as thin as bones. I answer him, or try to. My voice sounds strange.

"Stegi Stersi, B-9286." My mouth waters as it says the number, it is already thinking, at last, at last there will be soup. A lager creature is a creature of habit.

"Not your number," he says. "That time is over. What's your name?" he asks.

Phrases jump in my head. But none of them makes sense. Is this a seleckcja? *A trick?*

My name, it's on the tip of my tongue. My name. My name. What is it?

I am? I am? I am?

"Never mind, boy, can you stand?"

I don't know. They lift my legs.

I try.

I feel my heels press against the floor. My knees begin to grind. My bones press and crunch against each other. There is no cushioning flesh between them.

I start to rise. My legs begin to lever. I am standing. I am standing.

I hear my voice.

"Peter!" it says. "I am Peter!"

"Peter!" says the man. "I am Stefano."

I am Peter.

The words ring inside me.

I am Peter.

A carillon of bells.

His arm rises and he touches me. I feel his hand on my shoulder. It is a long time since I have been touched, my body flinches, expecting a blow.

"Don't stand, sit," Stefano says. It is surprising. His voice is gentle. His eyes look at me.

"Peter, can you make it outside?" the other one says. I stare at him. He is not as thin as I am. He wears the red triangle of a political. He seems to be crying.

"He's just a boy!" he says, but Stefano shakes his head.

"There are no children here. If he's survived this far, he's a man."

They link their arms together and make a sling. They lift me up and carry me.

"We need to get you out of here. There are still some of those bastard Blockaltesters left. Can you make it outside?"

Outside.

Outside.

I remember that word.

I see a chestnut tree.

There were streets. I think. And canals. And sunshine. And in autumn the leaves fell like gold coins that floated on the dark water of the canals.

"Is it still all there?" I whisper. "The outside?"

But they are struggling to carry me and cannot answer.

Around us there are piles. Piles of long matchsticks lying like people in the dirt. There are no rows now, no Häftlinge standing. There are no guards shouting. I close my eyes. I lift my face to the warmth and silence of the sun and feel it on my face.

I look around me. I see that the piles of matchsticks are men.

So many men.

All dead now.

Or dying.

I am still in Mauthausen, the place where . . .

The guards hold hoses in their hands.

"Stand! Stand! In fives. Two yards apart!" they shout.

The Häftlinge shuffle into place quickly, efficiently. They are old and young and ill and lame and injured. They were all different once—but in the guards' eyes they are all the same.

"Stand!" the guards scream.

The men crawl naked in the dirt, they struggle to rise to their feet. Some, just a few, jump up quickly, eager to please— but the old and the wise crawl as slowly as possible, saving each small second of energy. Judging it finely, this balance between rising as slowly as they can, but quickly enough not to be shot, or beaten—this balance between living and dying.

Every day I shuffle past the men standing like the naked skeletons of winter trees on my way to the quarry. Each evening when I return they are fewer. They are all naked. And it is freezing. At night the stars shine in a clear black frosty sky. The moon is clear. And they are beneath it. Standing. Like trees. In the morning the guards turn on the hoses.

"Stand!"

Each day there are less of them.

"Stand!"

Again and again.

It took the last man days to die. He stood up. He would not lie down. In the end they played with him. Let him rest for longer. Took bets. He thought he could win . . .

. . . but like I am, he just took longer to die.

The two politicals put me down. There is something soft beneath me.

"One of the guards' uniforms." Stefano laughs. "He won't be needing it now!"

The sun on my face feels like . . .

. . . a warm ball on my chest, bodies rising together like the whisper of the wind through the leaves of a chestnut tree, a burst of happiness like the taste of a strawberry. I remember Mouschi.

I feel my face smile.

The sun is real. I am not imagining it. It is here on my face.

"That's right, boy, you lie in it!" I open my eyes.

"They came!" Stefano says.

"We're liberated," says the other.

I close my eyes and smile. I've heard it all before, a long, long time ago. That word: Liberation. There was a room. And a radio. There was Anne. I had a mother then, and a father. We waited together, high in an attic, but no one came.

Except them.

It was sunny that day, too.

Stefano laughs.

"In the end, there were just too many of us!" he says. I listen to his voice. It has something strange in it. It has life in it. He must be a low number to be so strong. Has he done terrible things, too, like me?

"You sleep, boy," he says. "It's over now. The Russians gave us guns!"

"Do you know?" I whisper. "Do you know what they did?"

"We know, and soon the whole world will know, too," says the voice.

I sigh. I close my eyes. He talks of all the terrible things as though they are in the past, and not inside us.

I am thinking of Otto Frank. Of all the terrible things I did, leaving him to die is the worst. I can see him now . . .

We are standing together. It is the day they took my father. I cannot speak.

"What is left of him?" Mr. Frank says. "The clothes that came back were not his, the number on his wrist was not his."

"There's nothing left," I whisper.

"You!" he says. "You are what he has left. You will remember. You will survive. You will tell his story."

"Are we even men?" I ask. I am ashamed. I let my father go.

I let Mr. Frank go too . . . I walked away without him . . .

Can I call myself a man?

"Yes. We are men." Mr. Frank's voice is sharp and angry. "Never forget, Peter, it is *they* who are not men—all those who cannot feel shame. It is not *your* guilt or shame that matters. It is theirs. That is why you must tell your story."

And so I begin. In the only way I can, in words like footsteps, putting one in front of the other.

"Are you there?" I whisper to Stefano. "Can you hear me?"

"I'm here," he says, "I'm listening."

"They brought us here to Mauthausen from everywhere. Survivors. From Auschwitz and Budapest, from Plaszow and Buchenwald. All the Jews. They said we were vermin. A swarm of locusts. They kept on trying to kill us. But we kept on coming. They were our nightmare; now we are theirs. They gassed us. They beat us. They hanged us and machine-gunned us. They tried to walk us to death. But still, we kept on coming."

The man holds my hand.

"You're shaking," he says. "Hold on to me."

"They hosed us until we froze. They made us fall like dominoes down the steps of the quarry. They stood us by the wire and made us dance until we fell from exhaustion. And when we died upon the wire, dancing from the electricity twisting through our bodies, they laughed—and said—'He dances better dying!'

"Do you know this is true?" I ask him.
He squeezes my hand, "I know it now," he says.

"Some held hands and leaped to their deaths—they called them parachutists. And all the time they starved us. Worked us. Beat us. And still we came. Waves of us. They gave us typhus. And fever. And cholera. They made us carry our dead and leave them in piles. They fed our bodies through the chimneys and empty ovens. They spread the ashes of our bones upon their roads, and walked upon us. They made us wear the clothes of our dead, lest we should ever forget that we were next. They woke us before the sun rose. They stole our dreams. And still, we kept on coming."

"Yes! It was terrible," I hear the voice say, "and now it's over."

I have lived in fear, afraid not of death, but of a greater loneliness than that—of survival. Of having to tell when there is not a single other Häftling left. Not one to nod his head and say "Yes," or "It is true, they called us *Häftlinge* and *Untermenschen.*"

Only me, alone, with the disbelief in the eyes of the people outside.

"You're not alone!" he says. "There are others!"
    "Other Jews?" I ask.
    "Yes!"

Then I am not alone.
    I am not alone.
    I am only dying.
    I close my eyes.

"Peter!" they say. "Hang on, Peter!"

I smile.
    My name is Peter van Pels.
    I am Peter.
    And I have told my story.

"They've found some of the guards— look at that! They're kill-
ing them, Peter. They're beating the bastards to death with their
clogs!"

I will not open my eyes,
    I do not want to see their hatred.

Somewhere else, outside of here, there is a world where birds are singing.

In that world, I dreamed of freedom, of liberation.

And it has come.

"They're dead, the stinking cowards! Bloody hell, we're free."

"Can you open your eyes, boy?"

"I think he's going, mate."

"Not now! Not now, boy!"

"Can you hear me, Peter?"

"Listen, boy. Your people have risen up!"

I smile.

It is here, then. The moment I have longed for. Fought for. Watched others die for.

"You're free, boy. Free!"

Am I?

Can I ever be free of the pictures inside me? Of people standing in lines? Of a man putting a noose around his neck and jumping? Of God dying? Of bodies lying in piles like matchsticks? And of the truth that when there is nothing else, there is still the will to live? Driving us on, making us put one foot in front of the other. Me. In front of you. Because if I do not, I will die.

No more. I do not want any more.

Do you understand?

Are you listening?

Have you seen the dead lying upon the earth and drying—like roots pulled? Anonymous—like teeth.

I hear them whispering to me—the dead—I can see them.

"Boy! Open your lips. Here's water!"

The drops are sweet on my lips. Like a kiss.

"We're saved!"

But it is not the saved I see. It is the drowned. The dead. The nameless millions who already haunt me. I am sorry. I am sorry I pushed you down, I held my elbows out, I took the smallest rock so that you must pick up the heaviest. Where are the words for the nameless dead—for those who have already gone before me, and are calling me?

I am ready.

I am coming.

I am standing at the top of the stairs, reaching out my arms to my mother. I feel her name on my lips.

"Mutti?"

"He's going. They've had it once they call for their mothers."

I smile.

"He's smiling!"
     "Well, he's going to a better place, isn't he?"
     "So are we, mate, once we're out of here!"

She lifts her arms up for me . . .

"You are close, so close now," Anne whispers. "All stories must have an ending."

Pictures fill me.
     Merwedeplein in the snow . . . white blossoms shining against the evening sky in summer . . . a line of geese . . . a square patch of sky filled with stars.
     And Anne, words falling from her lips like leaves.

"Peter?" she says. "They cannot blow our words away."

The leaves of her diary lie scattered across the Annex floor.
     I am as light as a leaf now.

As ready.

"We are all dying," I hear Father say. "It's just a matter of timing."

If there is a heaven, then it is crowded with us. I take a breath and, with my last thought, blow the leaves of her diary up from the Annex floor. I watch them as they fly—up through the attic window, past the tree, past the birds and the chimes of the church clock. Beyond Anne, beyond me and Mutti and Papi and Otto and Margot and Edith. Up and up and up into the air, to where the hands of our enemies can no longer catch them.

Her words are written.

My story is told.

I am dying.

But others will survive.

Above us the words of millions hang waiting in the war-torn air like the last shreds of a burnt-out fire. Floating like pieces of ash. Soon they will settle. Some words will return with the living and never be spoken, but others will rise up in flames and cover the earth.

"Now do you believe in words?" Anne whispers.

Yes. I do.

I am so close now I can hear their voices.

"Peter!"

Joyfully, I lift my arms up higher. I raise my eyes, and see them: Mutti is barefoot and war-torn, her arms outstretched. Papi stands beside her, his glasses are twisted and broken but his mouth is still smiling. In his hands he holds a piece of worn pink silk. Anne and Margot cling to each other as their mother wraps her arms around them. Liese stands behind them, her head still shaved, waiting for me.

I search for Mr. Frank, but he is not with them. He is still among the living.

I let my breath go.

"Jump, Peter!" they shout together.

And I leap, up into their waiting arms.

———

Yes, I am dead now, but if you listen you can still hear me.

Wystawach.
Wake up.

Are you still there?
Are you listening?

Epilogue

After being in hiding for two years and one month, Peter van Pels was taken to a holding camp called Westerbork. From there he survived a three-day journey on the very last train from Holland into Auschwitz.

The experiences Peter has in the camps section of this novel are not documented, and are not, in that sense, real. They are reconstructed using other documented accounts. We do know that for a time Peter had a job in the postal department and that this would have meant he had extra rations, which he shared with Otto Frank.

For me, in this section Peter exists as an "everyman." He helps me to explain how the camps functioned, how they made a cold and systematic attempt to strip prisoners of their very sense of self, abandoning them to a world where even the most basic survival required that they learn to steal and cheat as they struggled to survive the attempts of the Nazi regime to eliminate them entirely.

Peter van Pels somehow managed to withstand seven months in Auschwitz and the loss of his father. Debilitated and starving, he was then forced on a death march through Poland and Austria to Mauthausen—a camp infamous for the inventiveness of its cruelty to Jewish inmates. Some historians think he may have died on the death march itself. Other records suggest he finally died in Mauthausen, sometime between being admitted to the sick bay on April 11, 1945, and the liberation of the camp on May 5. He was exceptional in that he survived so long.

He was eighteen years old.

Auguste van Pels was with the female members of the Frank family in Auschwitz and was transported to Bergen-Belsen with them. She was moved again in February 1945 to a slave-labor camp called Raguhn. Raguhn was shut down on April 8, 1945. Auguste was forced on a death march toward Theresienstadt. She died either on the way or shortly after arrival. It is possible that Auguste and Peter died within days of each other.

She was forty-four years old.

Hermann van Pels died during the Auschwitz October selections of 1944. He was gassed to death. His wife and son survived him by six months.

He was forty-six years old.

Edith Frank was with Margot and Anne and Auguste van Pels in Auschwitz until November 26, 1944, when Anne,

335

Margot, and Auguste were separated from Edith and transported to Bergen-Belsen.

Edith Frank fiercely supported her daughters in Auschwitz, at one point digging a hole into the sick bay, where Anne was being treated, to pass her food. She died on January 6, 1945, probably from exhaustion, starvation, and grief.

She was forty-four years old.

Conditions in Bergen-Belsen for Anne and Margot Frank were beyond belief. The camp system had broken down: there was no food, hygiene, or fresh water, and infection and illness were rife. The sisters stayed together and tried hard to look after each other. They slept in the same bunk, by the door, "the worst position, because of the cold," and there is a short account of the conditions they lived in by Janny and Lien Brilleslijper. Margot died of typhus. It is likely her body was simply added to a pile outside the door.

She was nineteen years old.

Anne Frank died alone in Bergen-Belsen, days after Margot. It is hard to imagine the depths of desolation she suffered at losing her sister, the last of her family. Hanneli Goslar believes Anne died of despair and loneliness as well as typhus. "There is no one left," she said across a fence in Bergen-Belsen. She died just days before Bergen-Belsen was liberated.

She was fifteen years old.

Otto Frank survived seven months in Auschwitz and the

ten days after the Nazis deserted the camp and left the survivors to fend for themselves in appalling and dangerous conditions. He eventually returned to Holland, where, after final confirmation that his children were dead, Miep Gies gave him Anne's carefully kept diary.

He made the decision to edit and publish it. The rest is history. Anne finally achieved her dream of "world-class" recognition. She had already, unbeknownst to her, written something "life-changing."

Her work and beliefs are protected and continued by the Anne Frank House and Foundation, which researches all forms of racism and genocide, including the recent rise of Islamophobia in Holland. They continue to encourage new generations to understand the nature and meaning of the Holocaust.

Otto Frank died in August 1980. He was eighty-one years old.

Fritz Pfeffer survived the October selections in Auschwitz and was transported to Neungamme camp, where he died alone, of enterocolitis, on December 20, 1944.

He was fifty-five years old. Charlotte married Dr. Pfeffer posthumously in 1953.

Liese, Peter's first "girlfriend," is a complete fiction. She exists as a way of representing the disappeared and disappearing Jewish citizens during the years of Peter's hiding.

Author's note

Writing historical fiction for the first time has proved a challenging task. Life within the Annex has been brilliantly portrayed by Anne; in Part One of my novel, her diary was my principal guide. Sometimes, in the interest of continuity of narrative, an event may have been moved. I hope avid diary readers will forgive me. I have tried to remain true to the spirit of the diary and the events that took place within the Annex.

The job of recording what may have happened to the occupants of the Annex once they arrived in the camps has been more difficult to unravel. In attempting to write about survival in Auschwitz and Mauthausen, I have at all times been guided by the testimony and evidence of camp survivors. I've read many books, but was especially moved by Primo Levi, whose clear-eyed testimony portrays without sentiment the reality of day-to-day life in Auschwitz.

My thanks to both Buddy Elias and Carol Anne Lee for reading the manuscript and making some invaluable suggestions.

Further information

BOOKS

Anne Frank, *The Diary of a Young Girl* (Bantam, 1993)
Miep Gies and Alison Leslie Gold, *Anne Frank Remembered*
    (Simon and Schuster, 2009)
Elie Wiesel, *Night* (Hill and Wang, 2006)
Markus Zusak, *The Book Thief* (Alfred A. Knopf, 2007)
Anne Holm, *I Am David* (Harcourt, 2004)
Primo Levi, *If This Is a Man* and *The Truce* (Abacus, 1991)
Art Spiegelman, *The Complete Maus* (Pantheon, 1996)
Peter Duffy, *The Bielski Brothers* (Harper, 2004)
Israel Gutman, *Resistance: The Warsaw Ghetto Uprising*
    (Houghton Mifflin, 1998)
Olga Lengal, *Five Chimneys: A Woman Survivor's True Story*
    of Auschwitz (Academy Chicago Publications, 1995)

DVDS
Anne Frank Remembered (2010) Documentary. Includes a
few seconds of the only film footage of Anne Frank.

WEBSITES
www.yadvashem.org
www.annefrank.org

Acknowledgments

MY THANKS TO:

Charlie Sheppard, my editor. Klaus Flugge and Sarah Pakenham at Andersen. Barry Cunningham at Chicken House. Margaret Raymo and Karen Walsh at Houghton Mifflin. Barbara Bradshaw, Paula Barry, Steve, Charlie, and Felix Bishop, Kate Dando, the Fiddes family, Danny Lee, Suzy Paul, and Rosemary Turan for their support and friendship. Andy Kelly, Gertjaen Brock, Bruce and Tess Blenkinsop for their help with information. Joy Court. Jem. Xa, Ella, and Alastair White for living with me as I lived through writing this . . .

8-14